PEPETELA is the *nom de plum_____* tur Carlos Maurício Pestana. _____ t to Portugal in 1958 to s_____ ___ent to France and then t_____ ___y and was involved in found_____ ___dies.

In the late 1960s he w_____ front and took part in the guerrilla war a_____ ___ial army. He was a member of the first MPLA _____ ___n to fly into Angola at the end of the war for independence.

Among other responsibilities, Pepetela has been Deputy Minister of Education and a leading member of the Angolan Writers' Union.

Pepetela is the author of many novels including *Yaka* (1984), which won Angola's National Literature Prize in 1986. The novels *Yaka* and *Mayombe* (1980) are also published in Heinemann's African Writers Series. *O Desejo de Kianda* (*The Return of the Water Spirit*) was first published in 1995.

In 1997 Pepetela was awarded the Camões Prize, which is the most prestigious literary award in the Portuguese-speaking world.

LUÍS R. MITRAS is a Mozambican-born South African, currently living in Lisbon. He has contributed translations from Portuguese-language writers and poets to various journals and anthologies.

PEPETELA

THE RETURN OF
THE WATER SPIRIT

Translated by Luís R. Mitras

Heinemann

Heinemann Educational Publishers
Halley Court, Jordan Hill, Oxford OX2 8EJ
A Division of Reed Educational & Professional Publishing Ltd

Heinemann: A Division of Reed Publishing (USA) Inc.
361 Hanover Street, Portsmouth, NH 03801–3912, USA

Heinemann Publishers (Pty) Limited
PO Box 781940, Sandton 2146, Johannesburg, South Africa

OXFORD   MELBOURNE   AUCKLAND
JOHANNESBURG   BLANTYRE   GABORONE
IBADAN   PORTSMOUTH (NH) USA   CHICAGO

This translation first published by Heinemann Educational Publishers in
2002

British Library Cataloguing in Publication Data
A catalogue record for this book is available from the British Library.

Cover illustration by Michelle Thompson
Author photograph by Bernd Böhner

Phototypeset by SetSystems Ltd, Saffron Walden, Essex
Printed and bound in Great Britain by
Cox and Wyman Ltd, Reading, Berkshire

ISBN 0 435 91210 0

02 03 04 05 06 07 08 8 7 6 5 4 3 2 1

Chapter One

João Evangelista was married on the day the first building fell. This took place in Kinaxixi Square. Afterwards they tried to find a cause-and-effect relationship between these two notable events, but this was much later, after the Luanda Syndrome had become headline news in the *New York Times* and the *Frankfurter Allgemeine*. Actually, it was five in the afternoon when João Evangelista got married at the registry office in Kinaxixi, and by six o'clock the building had collapsed. If a connection between these two things did exist it would seem that the cause was the wedding, not the building-on-a-suicide-mission. The problem is that things are never as clear-cut as we would like them to be.

João Evangelista came from a religious family. He was the son of Mateus Evangelista and the grandson of Rosário Evangelista. This surname that was so worthy of respect had originated with his grandfather, and that was because he was a pastor in an Evangelical church in Huambo. His father was born at the mission itself and he only left it as an adult, and that was to try things out in Luanda. João was born in the capital city, the offspring of his father's union with another church devotee. But at six he was sent to the mission in Huambo where his grandfather had preached and where his father was raised. He only returned to Luanda after he had turned twenty. His intention was to study engineering and he got himself a job so he could help his parents out. It wasn't long before he gave up his studies and that was because he couldn't reconcile his university timetable with that of his work. At least that was the reason he gave his friends. But to that reason we could also add his lack of interest in Maths and Physics, as well as the lack of teachers in the university, and the lack of buildings and equipment. João Evangelista was sick and tired of underdevelopment. That is more or less what he said to Carmina, his girlfriend at the time.

If his parents had been given any say in the matter, the marriage would never have taken place. Older people in the neighbourhood didn't think very much of Carmina. That's the reason why, even as a child, they had called her CAF – Carmina-arse-face. She really thought the sun shone out of her arse. By the age of twelve she was already bossing her widowed mother and her three older brothers. Admittedly, she was a remarkably intelligent girl, a fact which her teachers and schoolmates all acknowledged. But people also recognized that it took some guts to take control of a family at such a young age, never mind the fact that the mother was a sickly creature and the brothers were lazy-bones to the core. At fourteen she joined the Y – the Youth, the MPLA's Youth – and by the age of eighteen, when she met João Evangelista and had a sudden vision of her inevitable future, she was already an area leader. Old Mateus didn't think much of those who dabbled in politics, although he did understand that in times like these it was the only professional avenue open to a young woman who had more than a few ambitions and who was an expert in the art of being bossy. But the worst thing for the future father-in-law was the fact that the young woman was a disciple of the dominant new religion, and that was atheism. How could his son, educated in the best mission in the whole country, perhaps of Africa even, marry an atheist, a woman who feared neither God nor Satan? And worse than that, here was a woman who bossed men around, who complained about things, and who actually answered back.

2

But João was enthralled by CAF's sheer energy. To this day he does not know what Carmina saw in him, and it is probably true that she didn't even know herself. It was she, with her many political contacts, who had got him a better job in a state company, one that provided exceptional work conditions for its staff. And when they decided to get married she was able to 'acquire the keys' – as was the practice in those days – to a flat in excellent condition in a street called Cónego Manuel das Neves in a building right by Kinaxixi Square, that is to say, right in the centre of the city. Step Number Two, which was to register the flat in his name, was even easier: she had the most excellent contacts in the government. It was also she who offered João a computer as a wedding present. It is true that it cost her nothing. It landed on her as part of an order for computers made by the Y. It was only when the ordered computers were given out to those in charge that it was discovered that for the small amount of work they had to do half the order would have been more than enough. That is not to say that João wasn't touched by her thoughtfulness. Old Mateus grumbled: Since when did brides give wedding presents? And worse than that, this was a machine that served no purpose at all. Little did he know . . .

The first building came tumbling down not long after the cortège of cars transporting bride, bridegroom and guests to the wedding banquet left the registry office. It was a national event. All accounts agree on the details. There was no explosion. The sound of bricks crashing against the metal just wasn't there. Instead, there was a light musical tinkling sound, such as there would have been if the wind were to beat against a curtain made of thin glass strips. The walls disintegrated in a leisurely way and then slowly the furniture fell on top of the plaster and the sanitary fittings. This was followed by falling people and dogs, parrots and cats, nests of mice and of cockroaches, until eventu-

3

ally everything had tumbled to the ground. According to reports, the fall was accompanied by eerie lights across the entire spectrum of the rainbow. Something that was talked about a lot, although the press made no mention of it, concerned the huge bed that came tumbling down with a naked couple caught in the act of making love. There would be nothing remarkable about this if it were not for the fact that the two were men – well-known public figures, one in politics, the other in the world of arts. Two elderly people also tumbled down, more surprised than actually frightened. As one can see, it was only the building itself which was destroyed – reduced to rubble. Neither the people nor the animals that lodged with them, nor the furniture nor the household appliances, suffered so much as a scratch. It was something which had never been seen before: people falling from a seventh floor, landing on the ground and feeling as though they had come down with a parachute. There was even the case of the two well-known lawyers who had been engaged in a ferocious argument in a flat belonging to one of them. They continued to argue it out after they had landed on the ground – that is, until a journalist interrupted them to inform them of what had taken place. That was when, looking up, they both fainted with shock. I am sorry to have to add fuel to the fire of those who argue – *ad nauseam*, let's be honest – that lawyers are interested only in the sound of their own voices, but this detail cannot be denied since it is historically sound.

All in all the fall of the building had to be regarded as an event of national importance. Many suspected that a miracle had taken place because one of the impromptu fliers was a mother superior who landed on the ground with her habit flowing. A piqued nationalist reminded others right there and then that this country had never been well endowed with miracles. As far as we know there was only the Battle of Ambuíla, when the king of the Kongo was defeated and then

4

decapitated thanks to the work of the Virgin Mary who personally took charge of the Portuguese army – a commonplace act for this saint and her son, if we are to believe the tales with which we were force-fed at school during the colonial days. A miracle wouldn't be out of place in this age of little faith, when the government called itself Marxist – even though many suspected that their Marxism never went beyond the level of propaganda. In no time the miracle hypothesis gained fervent adherents, especially in the churches in Luanda, both in the ones that had already become traditional – those of European, American and African origin – and in the new, electronic sects.

The bride and groom got to know about the events at their wedding reception. They reacted differently to what had happened. CAF screamed: 'It was sabotage. We must catch the terrorists. They must be shot by a firing squad.' João Evangelista went pale, if that can be said of someone who is pitch-black, and thanked some deity from the days of his childhood. 'Just imagine if it had happened during the ceremony.' People couldn't stop talking about it all through the banquet and the party that followed. The bride's conjecture was soon refuted by others: 'There was no bomb. No one was hurt. If it was a bomb, and if it had the power to bring down a seven-storey building then Kinaxixi Square would be redder with blood than all the modern films that we see on TV.'

Old Mateus, who was sitting at the corner of the table, was extremely edgy. He kept nagging Dona Mingota, his wife and the mother of the groom, saying that it was time they be off since this was a fake wedding, one without any sort of religious ceremony. He said to his wife:

'These are sinful times. You'll see, many more things will happen. If my own son can marry a heathen . . . The only good thing that's happened is that now the wedding register has seven storeys of rubble on top of it. This marriage has ceased to be legally binding.'

'Oh stop it, Mateus. They'll make it legal again. Everything's always easy for her.'

But old Mateus Evangelista was really the odd one out at the wedding feast. Everyone else was having a ball, enjoying the good food and the wide choice of drinks, although the general preference seemed to be for the whisky and beer. Despite her young age, CAF was a distinguished member of the Y. And she was as good as elected to the Central Committee, for she would be standing as candidate at the next party congress. She had even come up with a campaign slogan: CAF 4 CC. It was for all these reasons that the Y had invested in the wedding. Goods were requisitioned from all the state companies that controlled the distribution of fish and seafood, meat and poultry, products from bakeries, breweries, and so forth. An indescribable quantity of goods was obtained at prices that were merely symbolic. The premises were supplied free of charge. The band was subsidized by the organization, and therefore played for free. To pay for the trousseau the bride invented a fictitious work trip to Rome – paid for evidently by the State. João Evangelista could only but be grateful to his young wife since he had been given a wedding feast worthy of a prince without having paid so much as a cent. And because she was a liberated woman he didn't even have to pay lobola – bride-money. He had sounded her out about this during their courtship, but her reply had been fierce: 'My parents will not sell me and I won't be bought. Only if it's the other way round. I am a socialist. To hell with these obscurantist traditions.'

Only if it's the other way round . . . The words lingered on in João Evangelista's brain and in the years that followed their wedding they loomed larger and larger in his mind. To what extent was he the one who had been lobala-ed, traded as cattle?

6

CAF did indeed make it to the Y's Central Committee and she was allocated a car, a sign that her social standing had moved up a notch. João Evangelista also made use of the car, especially when his wife was engaged in those three-day-long, night-to-dawn-the-next-day meetings. During these times he would take her to work and would pick her up because there was no way of predicting when those meetings would end. He would keep the car for the whole day. His job was dull and the prospects weren't great. And no one noticed his absences, in the same way that no one noticed the absences of the other staff. He would go to the *Morro dos Veados* – Stag Mound – or farther still to the beaches. There he would listen to music or read. Life smiled on João Evangelista, contrary to what his father had predicted, his father who was forever, even if indirectly, goading him to settle for an early divorce. The only negative thing about the marriage was Carmina's persistent refusal to have children, at least for the time being.

'When I make it to the Central Committee of the Party,' she would say.

'But then you'll be 40.'

'I'll get there long before that. There's plenty of time to get pregnant.'

One more reason for old Mateus to groan and moan: 'She's a child of Satan. She takes pills so's not to get pregnant. She won't even give me a grandchild. That house is a den of sin.' That was why he refused to visit his son, of whom he had been so proud until then. Not that Carmina noticed the absence of her father-in-law for she had other things on her mind, such as a mass cleaning campaign diarized for a Red Saturday, or making plans for a mass meeting in Caxito.

◆

7

A song, soft yet sorrowful, was growing from within the green and decaying water that for years had been allowed to spread next to a building under construction in Kinaxixi. It was meant to be a ten-storey building, but construction work had stopped at the time of Independence. First it was just a puddle growing next to all the iron of the foundations; it looked like something from a sewage pipe. That's where the tadpoles were born. Then came the frogs. The puddle began to grow and the plants that burst from within the water gave it a greenish appearance. Fish appeared. And the children took to swimming in it. Now and again there was news of a child who had disappeared while swimming on the edge of the lagoon, or of a child who was playing in the unfinished building and who fell in the water. There was also the case of a child who vanished under the water and who appeared in another place, with no memory of what had taken place or of how he had got there. The news would appear in the papers and, in no time, it would be forgotten. The song was far too soft. No one heard it.

◆

Time went by and people forgot about the collapse of the building, except for the former tenants who were worse off now – because of the housing shortage. But the authorities and the inhabitants really did forget. They didn't even seem to notice the rubble, which had never been removed, even though a foreign company had been hired to clean up the rubbish in the city. An enquiry was unable to identify the causes of the incident and the file was closed.

The building that fell was at the outer end of one of the rows of buildings around Kinaxixi, and so the rubble was not something one ever noticed. But years later a four-storey building fell. This one was right in the middle of a row of buildings around the square. There was the same musical tinkling sound as in the first case, the same colours of the rainbow, and the same scenes of people falling gently on to the ground, together with the furniture and animals; and again there was neither bloodshed nor any physical damage. But there was now a gap in the row of buildings and it was as though an incisor had been pulled out from an otherwise perfect set of teeth.

When it happens once people forget. But when it happens twice one can't really put it down to chance. The most ridiculous comments began to circulate among friends out drinking, in political discussions, during interviews, even in the middle of football matches. Well respected scientists were constantly asked for their opinions. They were as circumspect as philosophers, for they never really said anything: Yes, it was necessary to conduct some research, but the country was not in a position to conduct a serious investigation. A team of academics from a politically-aligned country in eastern Europe came visiting. They went sniffing around all the buildings in Kinaxixi, all the way up to Maianga. They listened to what the porters had to say, which for them was the key to the mystery, for in their country building porters all belonged to the secret police. But the porters in Kinaxixi were scarce and unprepared for a task of such weighty responsibility and the academics were unable to compile a satisfactory report. They returned to their country two months later, still as much in the dark as when they came, but well tanned thanks to all the time they spent on the beach, and with more than a few dollars in their pockets, and also with the promise that they would receive a medal for their efforts in carrying out an international proletarian mission in an undoubtedly dangerous area.

CAF despaired at the passive attitude of the police and the other authorities.

'It is quite obvious that they're saboteurs,' she would say with the force of conviction that only she knew how to give to the most trivial of sentences. 'Maybe the Americans are testing out a new product and they've passed it on to their terrorist friends. You've got to be blind not to see it.'

His wife's irascibility was the cause of some worry to João Evangelista. From what he gathered from their conversations she was foul-mouthed at party meetings. She ought to be more discreet; she shouldn't defend the sabotage theory with such vehemence. It could damage her chances of promotion. Imagine if they discovered that there was another cause for the collapse of the buildings. 'You'll lose your political credibility. You could even become a laughing stock, and that's the worst thing that can happen to someone in a position of authority. And what's worse, you went on TV to defend the terrorism theory. All we needed was for you to say that you had evidence of American involvement. Especially now that the country's beginning to make overtures . . .'

Carmina would tear out of the house, saying: 'Do shut up. You don't know anything about politics. Where you stand is at exactly zero degrees.' It wasn't altogether a lie, but João didn't like these comments which diminished him; he was, after all, the one who was male.

Then, all of a sudden, it was as if all the buildings in the city had fallen right on top of Carmina-arse-face's head. This was at the time that people began to talk of political change. People would come to visit and they would talk to João Evangelista about the so-called 'democratic opening-up'. CAF didn't even want to listen. 'Pack of traitors, imperialist lackeys, shameless followers of Gorbachev, shit-faced counter-revolutionaries.'

As these ideas began to grow – as they conquered those territories hitherto populated by secretive comments whispered in fear, and as the papers began to publish them – Carmina became thinner and thinner. Once again her husband worried about her, this time about her health. She didn't want to see a doctor. She said she was quite well. But her refusals were even starting to affect what they did in bed. 'I'm tired,' she would say. 'Tomorrow.'

It wasn't long before the climate of uncertainty disappeared altogether: the political régime really was going to change, despite Carmina's loud protests as the leader of the radical wing of the Y. It was made public that there had been official contacts with members of the armed opposition. CAF made an extremely violent speech at one of the sub-committees of the Y: she was trying to stir up open rebellion. She was becoming thinner still. Gone were those curves which had made her so attractive once, and even her rounded buttocks seemed to have become fleshless. João and his friends managed to convince her that she was digging her own grave, and that she could even go to jail for insubordination. 'When the river current's too strong the crab hides its head,' so goes an old Lunda proverb.

She eventually gave up on the idea, but each fresh item of news – now their daily bread – made her squirm with rage. It was decided to permit the existence of other political parties, to open the economy to capital from the private sector, and to make peace with the armed opposition.

'All we're doing is giving in,' she moaned, but only in the privacy of her own home because at meetings she was strangely silent. The spark in her eyes had gone out, an added reason for her husband's anxiety. One day while they were talking about a period in which no buildings had fallen down in Kinaxixi, she said:

'I always thought it was a secret weapon used by the Americans. Those buildings that used to fall, these political and economic changes, it's all tied up. Only the blind can't see the satanic hands of the CIA behind all this.'

João Evangelista worried still more: added to the extraordi-

11

nary gauntness of his wife was her growing anti-American paranoia. If a cat were to walk down the road in a manner which differed ever so slightly from its usual way of walking then she would accuse that cat of being a Yankee agent in disguise, one that was involved in some treacherous act of sabotage.

The new parties grew like the plants in the new lagoon of Kinaxixi. In this Carmina saw unmistakable signs of the Empire's strategy at work. She would read their manifestos and pamphlets, so alike in so many ways, and she would say: 'They have the scent of the CIA. They don't even bother to create different statutes. It is only the acronyms that change.'

João had to agree with her on this score, because their statutes did seem to be carbon copies of each other. But there was one thing Carmina was wrong about: the master mould had not been fashioned by the Empire, for they all copied the statutes of the one party which until then had been the only party and whose statutes they had merely revamped.

But not everything in this new political situation brought disadvantages for João Evangelista. With political activity at a frenzy and with everyone now trying out their hand at various businesses, his bosses took less notice of his absences, and he went weeks without so much as setting foot at work. CAF was almost unemployed as the Y had entered into a phase of being wound up. This had come about because of its need to curb expenses; the unlimited funds granted to them by the State had since terminated. She never felt like leaving the house and João was free to use the car for entire days at a stretch. He used the opportunity to drive around the city. He would come back with all the news and he used to relay it to Carmina so as to cheer her up and lift her out of her gloomy depression. But he had to censor the news very carefully because if, for instance, he said that he had bumped into a friend who was now a campaign worker for a new party she would turn wild.

'Sell-outs, traitors. They made themselves rich at our expense, but now they're fleeing the sinking ship. But they're wrong. The ship's not sinking. That's just American propaganda. They never could understand anything about this country.'

It occurred to João that, strictly speaking, it was quite true that the Americans had never understood anything about the country, although now the sentence was out of context.

And then one day – just as the season changes and the first rainfalls from the plateau clean everything and present us with an altogether different world – CAF shook her head as if to get rid of the evil spirits. Her eyes were shining as before and, in a very mysterious voice, she invited him to go out for dinner to one of the many restaurants that were opening up every day now, the first sign that the country was moving towards the so-called 'market economy'.

It was there, seated at the table in the restaurant, that she made her confession. Their meal had come to the end and the coffee and the cognac were being served. Her eyes were shining with delight once again.

'You know, I've been thinking. Everyone who is in a position of authority, or who's been in a position of authority, is now adjusting to the new ways. They do something here, something there. For example, Samuel – you know him, don't you? – he got rid of all the Ministry cars and was able to keep five for himself. He then gave a car to each of the directors to keep their mouths shut. As for Bisnaga, he managed to lay his hands on a set of military trucks and now he's building a most impressive private fleet. And there's that slimeball of a man, Joaquim Domingos, you already know all about him . . .'

João Evangelista had taken part in a discussion where he was told about Joaquim Domingos' latest acquisition. This artillery officer was known to his subalterns by a nickname that was as unoriginal as it was unflattering: Master Fart. Carmina's friends laughed at the story at the same time as admitting that he really had gone too far. This officer got hold of a Navy vessel – with cannons and all! – that was due to be declared redundant. He bought the boat for the token price of a thousand kuanzas, which at the time was just enough to fill a tank of a small car with petrol. Joaquim sold the cannons to a group of arms dealers who then took them to Rwanda – in Angola there now reigned eternal peace; that was the official view, at least according to government dogma. The boat was transformed into a fishing trawler in the Navy shipyards. This was done free of charge, because it is not for nothing that one is an officer. On the stern, where the cannons had been, he had quick-reaction harpoons installed; these were guided by lasers and other such state-of-the-art technologies. The last whales of the ocean were ready to be obliterated. The truth is that there was no escape possible for the poor sea breams and groupers in Mussulo Bay: off to one side went their heads, their entrails to the other.

'Three two one zero,' Master Fart would say when they managed to strike at a shoal. The results were visible only on the sonar screen because the bits of fish never reached the surface – unless one is referring to those bloodied remnants that followed the wake of the moving ship.

'Always on target,' bragged the artillery officer who had studied at the various military academies of socialist countries of eastern Europe. But the outcome was rather poor: on their return his fishermen always had to buy fish from others, that is, if they wanted some fish for their evening meal.

'The stories of corruption and embezzlement run into the hundreds and some are actually true,' continued Carmina. 'It's the end of an era and everyone's trying to save their skin while there's time. They've got their retirement pensions overseas in case the elections go wrong. And here am I, as stupid as hell, the last of the socialists. What do you think?'

João Evangelista merely thought, 'She's recovering from her depression,' and that gladdened him. At least she had stopped seeing enemies all over the place and she seemed to want to take up the fight, whatever it was. The role of a good husband is to support his wife. He held her bony hand and, very tenderly, he said:

'I think you shouldn't lose heart. You've got to carry on living, haven't you? Find some way of burning off that excessive energy you've always had. But are you really thinking of giving up politics?'

'That's why I'm asking you. I can become a businesswoman. That's what everyone is doing. I'm not talking about becoming an "economic agent" because that's just another name for someone's who's in the black market. Let's forget the word "capitalist", as we used to call it. Let's use the word "business-woman" since it doesn't offend anyone. The fact is, I'm a bit late on the scene because so many have moved in already and they've taken over many areas, but I'll still manage something. I could still fight for a place in the party's Central Committee, and that would guarantee that my name would be on the list of Parliamentary candidates for the election. That's what I'm asking you: businesswoman or politician?'

'Is it forbidden to be both?'

'Not any more, that's obvious ... D'you mean to say ... Wow, João, you're a genius! I've made up my mind. I'll do both things. It will be the perfect partnership. One activity supports the other.'

João Evangelista was left with the impression, one that would be with him all the days of his life, that he was totally redundant and that he had no effect on the decisions she took. He could see from the speed of her reaction that she had already come with the ideas well formulated, and the reason she had invited him for dinner was merely to celebrate this change in her life.

15

But João knew how to give her pleasure. He accepted her praise very naturally; he was allowing her to be the bountiful spirit. How she loved to be bountiful, especially if it didn't cost her anything. Carmina grasped his hand lying on the table and whispered:

'My great counsellor!'

João Evangelista was always touched by her displays of tenderness. He had often asked himself what a woman as brilliant and bursting with as much life as Carmina could have seen in him. He wasn't that different from her brothers, whom CAF generally referred to as 'idiotic', 'dim-witted' or 'lazy', and other similar compliments. He didn't regard himself as stupid, but he recognized that he wasn't exactly dynamic. He had discovered this about himself during one of those nights spent alone, when his wife was busy with her usual meetings. He had learnt the art of self-evaluation, an exercise that was quite common in the organizations he had been involved in, both religious and political.

That night he made a merciless self-assessment. It ended with his realizing that he lacked willpower, that he was too fond of his own comfort, that he had no taste for adventure or even for what is new. That is to say he was a nobody, someone destined to be a loser. Competent enough at sex, that is true, but that was no great feat in a country such as this. Apart from this admission of how much of a sheep he was – an exercise which, to be fair, all but exhausted him – he made only one decision: and that was to devote more time to the computer Carmina had given him as a wedding present and which he rarely made any use of. He never understood the connection between his less than flattering self-assessment and this pivotal decision, but the truth is that nothing in the world happens by chance. There certainly was a connection, but he was not sufficiently interested to discover it.

'That's how it is, darling. The Y is going to rent out some of the floors at the head office. I'll manage to get a good floor for my new company. You see, they're going to take a decision about it at the next meeting. I've got the support of all the comrades— Oh, I've already sounded them out. For the time being I'll just rent it, but later I may even buy it.'

'Dirt cheap, I bet.'

'It has to be like that. How else can we create a national business class? No one has the money to buy businesses or houses at fair prices.'

'But that'll make the State poorer, and we'll be poorer for it.'

'Sonny-boy, that old Marx explained it all ages ago. To create a business class someone has to lose money to them. How's this class going to make money? And it's always better if it's the State that's losing the money, instead of expropriating or stealing directly from citizens. Didn't we decide to move towards a market economy? So someone's got to pay. In real life one can't multiply the fish and the loaves. Or at least, the person who could do it is no longer around.'

João Evangelista wanted to remind her that the arguments he was using were the arguments she had used when they discussed these very things just a few weeks back. Actually, they didn't talk about anything else. It was most tiring. But to nit-pick about her old arguments would be a sign of sheer meanness, and that really wasn't his style. And Carmina was so happy. She had that same twinkle in her eye that she had had in the old days when she was about to make a speech that would demolish an adversary . . . the meanness would be all the more stinging. He merely smiled.

'So you really have made up your mind. What kind of company will it be?'

'Guess. What makes the most money?'

'Food, cars . . . Who knows. . .'

17

'You really are a genius, my dear. Import–export. For starters it will merely be import – what have we got to export, after all? But that's how it's going to be registered – it sounds better that way. I've already got a fax machine. And a phone as well. Computers I needn't worry about since whatever I need I'll get from the Y: it all comes with the rent. If someone needs a machine for draught beer I'll phone a friend overseas and I'll order it. I get the commission. Wine, rice, codfish, cars, dresses, anything at all. I know people all over the place so it won't be difficult. And what about the State, the biggest spender in this country? All I need to do is to convince a few ministers or first secretaries that my services are the fastest and the cheapest. The advantage is that I don't need to have capital. The overseas supplier is paid with the buyer's money and all I do is to put the commission aside.'

'Don't you need initial capital at all?'

'What for? My capital is the rented space, nothing else. The real capital exists in our brains and in the contacts we have. I've always maintained the habit of keeping the calling cards of all the people I've known for whatever political reason. And I have a diary that's always up to date. That's my capital – and the possibility of becoming a Parliamentarian and a member of the Central Committee. That's something with considerable weight. We all like to be on good terms with someone who's got a bit of power because we never know what tomorrow will bring . . .'

'If it was as easy as that we'd all be rich. Sorry – I don't mean to dishearten you . . . but I want you to see that reality's not at all like that.'

'Oh, I know what reality's like. It's not easy for everyone, of course. For me it's easier because I've got the contacts and the political clout. Perhaps I've lost a bit of it recently, but there's nothing that can't be regained. A boot-licker will get so far and no further, but I'm different – aren't you forgetting that the

18

Governor of the Bank is a friend of mine? And I'm on first-name terms with all the ministers . . .'

She was speaking in all seriousness and had thought about everything. And she would become a successful businesswoman, a member of the Central Committee and a Parliamentarian. The only problem was if her party lost the election and if the laws were changed. That was the only risk. But João was certain she could achieve her aims. And all of a sudden he felt ill at ease. He sent for another two cognacs to see if it cheered him up. He drank his in one gulp and the warmth of it did him good. But he did not forget what hurt: at no point in the conversation had Carmina associated him with her plan, despite the flattering remarks about his intelligence. Was she going to create her company all by herself, just as she had created her political career? Would João Evangelista continue with his boring job with no hope of promotion? Would he continue living off his wife's riches? They weren't very attractive prospects for a man, especially for one who didn't even have children that he could boss around. Or could it be that she was keeping the surprise for the end? That was it. At the end of the conversation she was going to say, 'Hey, partner, when are we going to draw up the deed for our company?'

Carmina went on speaking and speaking, but he was no longer listening to her. He was thinking of the advantages and the drawbacks of being her partner. The good life, working whenever he felt like doing it, and looking at the flies during work hours – all that would have come to an end. She would make him run off to the bank, to customs, to the harbour, heaven knows where, and she would treat him like an imbecile if he didn't sort out all the things he had to sort out in the time she had assigned him . . .

Being simply the prince consort was not something altogether lacking in virtue. But the fact that she didn't make an offer wounded his masculine pride. It would be so good to be able to say, 'I will consider your request,' only so that he could decline it with something like: 'Well, you know, I'm not given to those things. You're the one with the knack. I would much rather remain in the wings and give you some advice now and then.' And she wouldn't insist because she knew that these tiring activities were no good for him. And their marriage would remain as happy as on that day when the first building fell.

But she made no such suggestion. She paid the bill, said, 'Let's go,' and got up. Perhaps she would make it later at night, after they had made love. But not even then. Carmina, well fed and satisfied, turned over to the other side and drifted into her dreams about her import–export company and her anticipated ascension at the next month's party congress. And there was João Evangelista with his insomnia and the frustration that comes of being a wounded male.

Chapter Two

It was round about this time that João Evangelista developed a keen interest in computer games. Someone had given him a disk of 'The Roman Empire'. The objective of the game was to get promoted successively, to go from a simple centurion to Caesar, and also to conquer all the territories that had been Roman provinces two thousand years ago. The weeks preceding Carmina's election to the Central Committee were spent on a study of different strategies and tactics needed to win battles and chariot races and gladiators' combats.

Honório, his colleague at work and fellow resident at the Kinaxixi, came to warn him that his boss was furious with him, for he hadn't been to work for more than a month. What the hell had got into his boss? He had never worried about these things before. Actually, he had to drop by the company because the salaries were being paid out, so he took a break from the game and went with Honório to face the wrath of his boss. This he overcame without too much difficulty.

'You know, boss, my salary's not enough for my basic needs. I have to do a few odd jobs as well. We don't know what the future holds and my wife has added risks now that she's a member of the Central Committee.'

The director, who was directly responsible to a minister who was also a member of the Central Committee, immediately understood the reasons, especially the last one.

'But you've got to come now and then. Otherwise the workers will say that some are more privileged than others, and during election time that's not a good thing. But tell me – what sort of odd jobs are they? I'm curious to know how I could add a few cents to this meagre director's salary.'

João Evangelista said he was helping his wife to set up a company. 'She's the owner. All I'm doing is helping out, with advice – and doing the groundwork. You know what it's like.'

But of course he did. Comrade Carmina was a lady of enormous capabilities and a most dynamic party member at that. This company, his boss insisted, was bound to be a success. 'And do give my regards to your most esteemed wife.'

João Evangelista left his workplace feeling a little guilty. This was not so much because he had lied, for he had ceased to have scruples about such things when he left the mission and decided, once and for all, to forget about sin; it was such a limiting concept. Rather, it was for having used Carmina's political position as something with which to intimidate the director. His boss wasn't such a bad person, after all, and he had always let him be, to the point that the company was sinking into bankruptcy, the only solution for which were the constant injections of State cash.

He forgot his guilt and his worries as soon as he turned on his computer and began to fight those terrible Scythian horseriders. A wedge formation was of little avail against them, as were the slow-moving infantry legions. The Scythians called for a new strategy, one he had to invent since the game offered none. Joana, the maid, came to give him a message. He said yes without even listening to what she had said, for he had to mobilize a new army as he had to attack disdainful and impregnable Scythia once again. And there appeared Carmina as if in a whirlwind.

'Hello, darling. I asked her to tell you lunch was ready. Didn't you hear? Good morning – I didn't even greet you. I'm in a hell of a hurry – I've got to go immediately after lunch. I've got lots to tell you. I'll tell you during lunch.'

João Evangelista had to turn off his computer and mull over his next moves during the meal, at the same time as pretending to listen to Carmina's non-stop conversation. Except that this time it was different; she really wanted an answer. After a second attempt, already half-angry, she raised her voice:

'Jeez, can't I even speak to you any more? Have you lost your brains?'

'I'm sorry, I'm sorry. It's just that today I went to work . . .'

'And what about it?'

Like a child who's caught dreaming about the beach in the middle of the maths class, he had to think of a quick excuse to explain his persistent distractedness. The best thing was not to say anything, but to hint at things instead.

'Well, there are a few problems there. But the director sends you his regards and wishes you the best of luck with your company.'

Carmina calmed down and repeated her question. 'Overseas Import-Export. Is that a good name for the company? Yes or no?'

João grimaced. 'You know, that name's still got a whiff of colonialism. In the old days we were "overseas"; the Portuguese were the ones from the "Mother Country" – although "overseas" means nothing more than from the other side of the sea. But if anyone dared to say that Portugal was overseas, there was a chance that that person would get arrested for having insulted the nation of King Alfonso I. A country like that deserved the more dignified name of "Mother Country".'

'I'm aware of all that. But a company needs to have a provocative name. And this is it. What we're seeing now is a re-appropriation of the colonial heritage. There are plenty of

23

people around who miss the old days; they say people were better off before Independence. That's why to call a company "Overseas" at this point in time will strike a few chords with people. And it really is about moving goods from one side of the sea to the other side.'

'Since you've already decided I don't see why you're asking for my opinion.'

'But your opinion is important. Even if you're not always right, like this time. Admit that you got it wrong this time.'

'You've got a political career. And you should do what you can to maintain it. If there's one thing people still hold on to in this country it's nationalism. Sometimes they're confused, sometimes they're not; they complain about everything, but they remain nationalist. You're toying with their nationalist feelings. Don't complain later when you need their votes.'

'What name do you suggest, then?'

'Who knows? Maybe give it the name of one of those fruits that's so much in fashion. There are so many things with names like Cherry, Mango, Banana, Pineapple. How about *Múcua*?'

'You're kidding! That's settled – it's definitely "Overseas". We've got to convince ourselves that we are the Mother Country and that the others are overseas. We should reclaim the nationalist sense of the words – you're right about that. All the advertising slogans will suggest that nationalist sense of the name. "Overseas" refers to the others. And my company's going to take us to those savages in Europe who are hanging from the trees by their tails – those savages wouldn't even be walking if we hadn't discovered and civilized them.'

Once again Carmina twisted things in her favour, thought João without any bitterness. He didn't answer back. It just wasn't worth it to insist. He quickly finished his meal and returned to his computer.

Many battles later, with the Carthaginians suffering deadly

24

attacks from the Roman legions commanded by Scipio Africanus, and after two of his fleets had sunk in the *mare nostrum* that was the Mediterranean, that was when Joana ran into the office. 'Another building's fallen down. I think it's Mr Honório's.'

João walked over to the window from where one could see the back of the building where Honório lived. The entire thing lay on the ground. The dust had still not settled and the building seemed to be immersed in a thick mist. People were shaking the dust off while they looked for each other and for their belongings. João went on staring: 'I've got to go over there and see what's happened to Honório and his family, but not now – it's not worth it because he's probably at work at the moment; much rather finish off those blasted Carthaginians and avenge my two sunken fleets.'

He returned to his game and forgot about the building that was known as the Cuco Beer building, and which had disintegrated to the sound of musical notes.

◆

The song, soft yet sorrowful, born from within the green lagoon next to the building under construction, ascended one tone along the scale. The building already had tenants. God knows where they came from. The lower floors were the first to be occupied. Because there were no walls they used cardboard and plywood divisions. They improvised with ladders since the original stairs had been left unfinished. One day it was discovered that there was light in one of the flats. The building had been connected to one of the lamp-posts in the street. More homeless people were drawn into the building. More flats were getting to be occupied. Next to it the lagoon grew, and so did the fish within it. The experts on the matter said that the fish from the lagoon were tastier than from Funda. I swear I never tried any such fish. A child fell from the fifth floor and drowned. His body was found three days later. The story was reported in the press. And suddenly the city discovered that the building was occupied all the way up to the top floor, and that to get there these people risked their lives by climbing up makeshift ladders. There was such a housing shortage in the city that the authorities did not have the courage to throw them out into the street. Where would they be sent? More flats now had electric lights. Next to the building, in the lagoon, the song soared up but no one heard it, not even the journalists who went there to report on the story of the drowned child. But it had been there for a long time. Perhaps even from the beginning of time. I recognize it now, with all the useless wisdom of old age. Useless, because it is like the song: one only hears it when it is too late.

◆

The game ended late in the afternoon. Rosy violet hues were already washing over the blue of Luanda's sky. João decided that he was going to find Honório. Maybe he needed some help.

He turned at the street corner and walked into Kinaxixi Square. The building that had an advertisement for Cuca Beer right on top of it had been one of the tallest in the square. It was now a mound of rubble and furniture, all of it covered with a thick coat of cement dust. The square was crowded with thousands of people. The tenants were looking for their belongings on top of the rubble. Sometimes this gave rise to pitched battles because many of the objects were identical and were claimed by various families. Around them were inquisitive bystanders who had come from all parts of the city. It wasn't easy to find Honório in the midst of all this confusion. First he found a detective sergeant accompanied by all his men who were

26

taking measurements and conducting an in-depth investigation. It was just like any other police investigation – at least in the early stages, when so much was promised.

João knew the detective, who greeted him courteously. There was nothing new to report, he said. There were no new leads. It was the same situation as for the other buildings. But then, just as he was leaving, the detective stood almost as if to attention and said: 'We shall discover the criminal hand that's behind all this.'

This certainly placed him in Carmina's group, for she was the one who defended the existence of a Machiavellian sabotage plan. After João had repeatedly asked him whether there were any signs pointing to sabotage, he shook his head sadly. 'Actually no. But we shall find it, because it *was* sabotage. We are in absolute agreement about this.'

João couldn't be sure who it was the policeman was in agreement with. It wasn't possible that he could be referring to Carmina. Or could it be?

There were Honório and his wife searching for their belongings on top of a mountain of rubble. That mountain was what remained of their flat, except that ten other flats had somehow got all mixed together, each of the flats that was below the other. This certainly created a few difficult problems to sort out.

'Can you believe it, all the neighbours used to buy the same type of fridge. This was at the time when there was practically only one make on the market. That's why as soon as we discover a fridge, before we even open it, all the neighbours have to tell us what's inside it. The one whose contents more or less correspond to what they said was there is the one who keeps it. This isn't too difficult. But what about the televisions? There's nothing inside it to distinguish it from another. That's when all the endless discussions start. Each person tries to point out some defect or some scratch which identifies it as their own. But we're

27

quite organized in this section and may just sort everything out.'

'It will take a long time.'

'Weeks. This will take weeks.'

'And in the meantime, where are you going to live? With the housing shortage being what it is . . .'

'We have no idea— look, Margarida, isn't that bit of furniture ours?'

The wife went to check out some sitting-room chair that was becoming visible amidst the ironwork and the bricks, all thanks to the efforts of two women who were sweeping the dust off the mounds. It would have been better to use some sort of massive vacuum cleaner because there was sand and cement dust by the ton. Honório ran in that direction so that he could help defend his wife who had already got involved in a row with a neighbour who also claimed to be the owner of the item of furniture.

'I'll be back,' shouted João as he moved away. He left the mountain terrain, for it was a dangerous place to be because one could step on some hidden remnant of ironwork. He found himself among a group of four people who were collecting dust into glass jars. The oldest person in the group taught at the Faculty of Science; the others were probably her students. He recognized her from TV; she had once spoken about the preservation of turtles. These were in danger of extinction because they were mercilessly hunted down for their shells which were used in the making of traditional handicrafts.

'Have you found anything interesting, ma'am?'

The lady, absent-minded as are most scientists when they are at work, must have taken him for an official of sorts, for she gave him a detailed description of what she'd discovered, one that under normal circumstances would not have been justified. It also needs to be said that the many years spent at the mission had given João an air of respectability not usually seen among the people of Luanda.

28

'We are just collecting cement dust to analyse it. It's obvious the problem has to do with the cement, like in the other cases. It goes back to its original state, as though the water had suddenly been removed from it. It even happens to reinforced concrete. That's why the buildings fall down. It's the only element that is altered. Everything else – bricks, iron, china, pipes – remains unchanged. That's why we decided to study this dust which is all that's left over from the cement.'

'But aren't you a biologist, ma'am?'

'All the departments are studying the phenomenon. Each one from its particular area of interest. Who knows if we won't find some micro-organism that is responsible for the transformation of the cement, or, at least, for the removal of the water. Everyone is here, those trained in chemistry, in mathematics, in the earth sciences, physics. Each one is studying this phenomenon from their own vantage point. Is the Luanda Syndrome of biological origin? Or is it chemical? Or does it have to do with physics? We have to explore all the possibilities.'

'Of course, of course. But if the buildings fall because the cement returns to its original form, that doesn't explain why the fall is so gentle . . . why no one gets hurt.'

'The experts on physics are studying that very aspect. Is it possible that the law of gravity operates differently in Kinaxixi? Or does it cease to operate at all from a certain point in time? Questions. All we have are questions. The fact is that no one has been able to explain anything. That is why we are researching. And we have to study it from all possible angles.'

João wished her success with her task, and he spoke in all sincerity. If anyone deserved respect it was these sort of people who insisted on studying things out of love for learning, and who knew perfectly well that they had little to gain from it, and that the results they obtained from their investigation probably wouldn't even be used by those who ought to take decisions

29

based on such results. It was important to respect the dedication of these misunderstood scientists and he made the esteem he felt evident to the academic. He walked back towards Honório's mound. But before he got there, and without wanting to, he was drawn into listening to a religious sermon. This he followed to the end.

A bespectacled mulatto was on top of the mound of rubble making an inflammatory speech about how this was all God's punishment, how the residents in the building with the Cuca Beer advert had refused to pay their tithes to the Church, and how it was now His turn to laugh, and laugh He did.

'Well I did warn ye that the ways of the Lord are inscrutable, but ye would not believe. Ye chose to continue with your licentiousness, your luxury and selfishness, and would not help to build the Temple of the Lord, the Church of the Lord. You had it coming,' said the street artist changing his tone, and perhaps his choice of language too. 'Now that you've lost your shacks you can't shack up with your neighbour's wife, because the Lord has brought you down with his divine wrath.'

Ever since his days at the mission, João had retained a certain admiration for those who had the gift for rhetoric. That's why he lingered on to listen to the prophet of doom, even though it seemed to him that his tone of voice was too shrill for João's more attuned ears.

Those that ought to be listening to him, for they were the butt of his harsh words, were too busy searching for things in the mounds of rubble. But two onlookers standing behind João had this to say:

'These guys are the pits. They'll use the slightest opportunity to make propaganda for their sect. And as for our Church . . . it does nothing. It is so comfortable in its seat of power, so fat and gilded, that it can't even move.'

'We should go to the church of Our Lady of Mount Carmel

30

and alert a priest. We have to beg him to do something. This is not like the old days. There's competition now and these people are so full of energy that they gain followers. And these electronic sects are growing at an alarming rate. In no time they'll be bringing their sound equipment and everyone in the square will have to listen to their speeches, whether they like it or not.'

João saw the two middle-aged gentlemen, impeccably dressed in suits and ties, walk down in the direction of the church of Our Lady of Mount Carmel. His father, Mateus Evangelista, would have said: 'There go the two papist crows to hand in their report to their papist boss, the one who worships idols made of stone.' His father had retained the vocabulary and the enmity of previous centuries, from those days before ecumenism when Catholics persecuted Protestants and tried to prevent them from entering Angola. They still made low moves, but the in-fights had become more civilized. But not Mateus; he had not changed the way he talked. In the meantime, the prophet continued to harangue, not in the least disconcerted by the disinterest shown by the shadows that wandered among the rubble.

And João Evangelista remembered the dream he'd had the night before. He remained there, staring at the wreckage inundated with people, as he recalled the strange sensation he had felt when he woke up. He was in an unfamiliar place. It could have been a city or a town; he couldn't be sure. All he knew was that there was a line of destroyed buildings; some were still burning. He soon realized that it wasn't the same type of rubble as in Kinaxixi. It was dead quiet in the street; only a few muffled sounds could be heard. No one was running. There were many bodies lying on the ground. He couldn't be sure whether they were dead or not, although this was something that didn't seem to have mattered to him at the time. It was night-time and there was a thick mist, almost what they call woman-rain, which is

31

really a drizzle and quite annoying at that. He was cold. So he picked up a body that was crouched in the foetal position on the ground. He put the body on his back and began to carry it. Slowly it dawned on him that the body he was carrying was that of a woman. Thin, and so light that to carry her required almost no effort, but it was also warm. That meant that she was not dead. But it was as though she were – frozen, inanimate, mute.

He walked and walked, down along the road and out into the night, always within that kingdom of silence, but warmer for it with that woman-plume on his back, until he eventually reached another town or city. He wasn't sure which, but it also had a road. There were people walking slowly from one side to the other like zombies. There was the same silence of the mist as there was in his city, although here there were soldiers. The only people running were the soldiers, but without making any noise. 'Has the war ended?' he thought to himself. Why are there soldiers and dead people if there is no war? The voice containing the answer came from behind him: 'But has it really ended?' What the hell? How could they have answered him if he hadn't even put the question in words? He was sure of the question, but all he had done was to think it. The voice of the woman had awakened something in his insensitive being. It wasn't the voice of an old woman. But how could she be so feint if she weren't old? For the first time he felt the weight and the shape of what he carried behind him. All of a sudden, he had the desire to return home – a home he was sure he possessed in that street he'd come from.

He turned halfway round. The voice behind him was sharper: 'Where are you taking me?'

'I'm taking you to my place,' he said.

And she replied, 'I can walk. I'm not wounded. I don't even know why you're carrying me.'

He said, 'I'll take you, just like I brought you.' And he

continued to walk, and the woman's filthy body began to acquire volume. But it remained light to carry, even though he was now beginning to grow tired.

She insisted again, 'Why did you carry me?'

He really didn't know. Or better still: it was an impulsive act born out of no real motive, except for the one he later discovered: 'I was cold and I thought you were dead.'

'The dead don't keep people warm,' she replied and he said to her, 'That's what I found out, when I stopped being cold.'

'Put me down on the ground,' she demanded. And that's when João Evangelista woke up.

He felt that same sensation of emptiness as he gazed at the mounds of rubble. The night, fortunately without any mist, was falling over the hundreds of people who were looking for their belongings in the dust, and the thousand other bystanders like him who were getting in the way. He went towards Honório. He was having an argument with two women who were both holding on to a pot; he was probably trying to calm them down. João wasn't going to waste time and so he took him to the side and the two women were left to fight over the pot.

'Sleep at our place for the next few days. I'm sure Carmina won't mind.'

'We'll sleep right here. To keep an eye on our things. Have you seen all the people looking to see what they can get? If we go, we'll be left with nothing.'

'What about the police?'

'They say they're going to seal off the area. But they'll be the first to steal – you know what they're like. Don't worry. The Red Cross is going to bring some tents. We'll sleep here. The residents have already organized themselves. We'll take turns to keep watch.'

'And food?'

'That's going to be a bit more difficult. They spoke about a collective kitchen with food from Mission Aid. It seems they have some supplies in their warehouses. But that's not going to happen today. These things take time.'

'I'll bring something. Better still, why don't you come for dinner at our place? If you're all going to take turns to keep watch then you don't have to worry.'

'Er . . . I'd rather stay. If you wouldn't mind sending somebody over with something; I'd prefer that. Something simple. All this has killed the appetite of the building's biggest glutton.'

João was working out the time and he guessed that Joana, the maid, must have already left. He ought to have thought about this before. How was he going to cook for his friends? There was no way Carmina would do it; she would want to eat as soon as she arrived home. Dinner was already made but it wasn't enough for four people. It would be up to him, of course. An omelette or a scrambled egg sandwich was quite in order. Crikey, he was not running a restaurant and hadn't Honório said that something simple was enough?

'All right, I'll see to it. But where are the children?'

'They were sent to Margarida's uncle's house. The place is minute, but he insisted on looking after them. That's one less worry for us.'

Honório returned to the rubble – to the searches and the inevitable fights with the neighbours. Carmina was right: we have to find a house to live in. These apartment blocks just create conflicts; everyone lives on top of each other like the Europeans do; it doesn't go well with our African way of being. Even more so when they begin to fall down; it's just like Sodom and Gomorrah.

João continued to walk, trying to work out in his mind the solution to the predicament of dinner for Honório and his wife. It could be the pizza in the freezer. All he had to do was to warm it up. 'That's it. No problem. Pizza and beer. That's been

34

sorted out . . . We really have to find a house as soon as possible. Our building is too close to all this. All of a sudden . . . Cross my fingers: even to think about this gives me the creeps.'

He noticed that the two Catholic custodians of morals had managed to drag a priest along. There he was, hurling smoke from a censer – or whatever that Russian samovar-style teapot was called – at the ruins and the rubble. The two gentlemen followed him at a close distance, their hands together as if in prayer. There was no sign of the speech-making prophet. In his place was the speaker from a newly-created political party who accused the single-party government of being responsible for this catastrophe, for it had contributed nothing towards the upkeep of the buildings. Any and everything could be used as election propaganda, for the elections were drawing close. If Carmina had been there the confusion would have been greater, because she wouldn't have tolerated listening to these sort of gratuitous accusations without doing her best to strangle the other speaker – or at least shutting him up for a few months.

Evangelista watched the fumigating priest again and he was perplexed. He almost went up to ask him what purpose it served to throw so much smoke over what was already done. Much better to fumigate the buildings that were still standing. Perhaps it would prevent their falling. He had to tell his father about it. He would start shrieking:

'They are hallucinating and they are superstitious, as if the smoke could ward off evil spirits. Witchdoctors use smoke, in fact, but they are pagans and we have to forgive them for that. Don't the papists know that demons can only be warded off with good actions and good thoughts?'

He thought it better not to ask anything. In a way it was because he felt sorry for the priest who seemed a bit lost in the midst of all this chaos. Harassed by the two pious gentlemen, criticized for having allowed the Church to be taken over by aggressive sects, he'd probably picked up the first object he'd laid eyes on. Perhaps they were even the trappings for the last rites. It was obvious he was doing something to escape from the sharp tongues of the two gentlemen in suits and ties, evidently influential people in the Church. And in difficult times any priest will have to defend his position and livelihood because in this country there are no saints.

He returned home, took the pizza from the deep freeze, and warmed it up in the oven. Carmina had still not returned; far too busy she was with her election campaign and building up her company, Overseas Ltd. He left her a note: 'I am at the rubble of the Cuca Beer building, together with Honório.' He took dinner to the couple.

He didn't see the priest this time, but he couldn't be sure if he was gone because there were thousands of people in the square and hundreds in that corner where the Cuca Beer building had once stood. He did, however, find the politician, who was repeating the same speech to a group of five people, and was by now already half-hoarse. He stopped to look for Honório and he caught a few of the sentences uttered by the speaker: Because the arrogant and despotic party in power demagogically established ridiculously low rents in all these buildings that had been abandoned by their former owners – settlers who fled to the Motherland – the State felt under no obligation to symbolically invest the money it earned from the rents in the upkeep of these homes, the consequence of which was that the buildings fell down from sheer tiredness and in revolt from being undervalued, for how could we admit that in an African capital of some dignity that such fine apartments could have such low rents, unless the intention was to demoralize, psychologically speaking, other more modest buildings, a scandal which would only end if they voted *en masse* for his party, the name of which he gave, but which João had never heard of, because no doubt it had been created only in order to benefit from the state subsidy he was so critical of and it probably only had two members, the speaker and his wife.

'If that! I bet your son won't even vote for you, you crook.' But João quickly came back to his senses: 'I'm becoming like Carmina. I should be tolerant of these up and coming parties.' That's when he met Honório and Margarida, which immediately made him forget the fiery candidate for political office.

He returned home, leaving his friends to their more pressing tasks. On his left was the market of Kinaxixi, thick and compact in the dark. It was full of people looking at the débris and the goings-on. Close to that spot must have been the place where, 30 years before, they cut down the tree of the Water Spirit, during the time when they built the square. The entire area had once been a lagoon and there had been a sacred tree which was cut down and which shed blood from its stump for an entire week. He'd heard the story, right there in an esplanade in Kinaxixi, when he had once sat down – with the greatest respect – at a table where there were two writers present, Luandino Vieira and Arnaldo Santos, both of them extremely knowledgeable about things to do with Luanda. As expected, the two men spoke about their childhood days in Kinaxixi, even though Luandino was really from Maculusso, which is next door. He was the one who told the story:

'Do you remember, Arnaldo, when the huge tree shed tears of blood for seven days? No one knew if it was from the pain of being felled or in sorrow because they had taken the lagoon away from the Water Spirit.'

Arnaldo Santos, a gentle person with a gentle way of speaking, smiled into his beer glass and calmly explained it to João: 'The land around the lagoon was all red, and the liquid which

37

came out from the stump that was cut was perhaps the sap mixed with the products that the roots had sucked from the red earth, and which people took to be blood.'

But Luandino cut him short: 'Stop trying to explain the inexplicable.' He spoke very earnestly and there was an indescribable smile on his face. 'It was blood. The people said so. You see, the Water Spirit's tree cries blood when it is cut.'

'It must have been in this place,' thought João as he walked home, 'that the Water Spirit's tree stood so majestically.' And even though it was a warm evening he felt a cold shiver whistling down his spine. He stepped up his pace.

Chapter Three

When the election results became known, Carmina didn't throw a big party to celebrate her new status as Parliamentarian, as she had planned to do. It wasn't opportune to do so because the defeated party had not accepted the election results and once again war had broken out. At first it was a low-intensity affair. For months the rebels marched on the district capitals with their armies in camouflage and expelled and persecuted the district commissioners who were favourable to the party that had won the elections. And then, for three days, it all blew up in Luanda, and with great violence at that.

It was around this time that João Evangelista had discovered a new computer game, one to do with creating civilizations. It was a lot more complex than the Roman Empire one since it involved founding cities, arming them, making them develop through science and economy and even through political processes, such as revolutions and changes of régime. It involved conquering other civilizations until a world-scale empire could be formed. While the streets of Luanda suffered bombardment he would lock himself up in his study trying to conquer Rome or Babylon, at first with catapults and later with cannons and armoured vehicles.

Carmina spent her days dialling numbers on the telephone to try to make sense of the way events had unfolded, and to communicate with others in positions of leadership who, likewise, did not know anything because those who were fighting out on the streets were not led by anyone in particular. She would come to give João the latest news, some items more false than others, and he wouldn't even interrupt his game; he listened distractedly to her saying that an enemy base had been destroyed – he was far more worried about carrying out his own war on the computer. CAF despaired at her husband's passivity, but she did not have the force of will to criticize him for it. She chewed her nails at the prospect of their being defeated and chased out of the country. Her main concern was to find a place on a getaway plane if things went wrong. But the planes couldn't even take off for the air space had been closed, and she wasn't even sure if, when the time came, she would still have her privileged status. That's why she would phone this person or that in order to try and secure a passage out for herself. The problem was that no one knew anything, not even about the evacuation plans. She would linger for a few minutes in the study watching João who had taken refuge in his empire-under-construction, and then she would go to the window to try and guess how the situation would eventually unfold. Then she would be back at the phone. The generals were unreachable and those who had stayed at home knew as much as she did.

'Why did we disband our army? Why didn't we act like the others who kept theirs? Naïveté, it's all naïveté.'

Her husband mumbled some distracted answer: 'That's democracy. But what I should really do is create a revolution and set up a republic, but that'll make me lose time and the cities will rise up and then the Russians will come and attack me, and those followers of Stalin are hellish because they'll never stick to the rules of any peace accord. What I really must do is make more cannons and leave this despotic monarchy as it is, because that's the best system for war – at least there'll be no internal revolts and that will allow me to think of strategy on a world scale.'

And Carmina would go and listen to the BBC newscasts and those from the Voice of America. Perhaps they knew more about what was really going on in Luanda, unlike she who was on the ground.

By the third day it became obvious that the rebels had been defeated and there were ecstatic telephone calls. The neighbourhood groups, created by former military personnel and supported by the police, had been able to achieve victory. She opened the bottle of champagne that had been kept in the fridge. She invited Honório and Margarida, who lived in a tent right in the heart of Kinaxixi Square. The four were going to celebrate. João was forced to interrupt his game in order to receive his friends. They told them about the days of terror they had spent living in a tent with twenty other people, and which offered them no protection from bullets. Fortunately there had been little activity in that area, although they could hear gunshots everywhere.

'You should have come here,' said João. 'At least we've got walls.'

They replied: 'We were too scared to cross those two hundred metres. We preferred to stay put.'

Gunshots could no longer be heard and a champagne cork wouldn't frighten anyone, would it? The fact of the matter is that at the exact moment that they were celebrating victory another building tumbled down, close to where the first building had fallen. They didn't realize this at first, which gave them enough time to drink the champagne. It was the screams coming from outside that directed them to the small balcony at the back of their flat. They could see the wreckage on the other side of the square through the space left open by what had once been the Cuca Beer building.

'Don't you see that it's sabotage?' yelled CAF. 'And it had to be at the moment of victory.' The other three didn't set much

41

store by these suppositions, which were more than denied by the evidence available. The three just gazed at each other. But the old Carmina rose to the surface. She railed at the capriciousness of the democratic system. They had been naïve to believe in international guarantees.

'Who could be conned by the promises of the American imperialists? They cooked up this whole dirty business of getting their protégés to take control. I wouldn't be at all surprised if the 7th Yankee Squadron were waiting outside, ready to bombard Luanda. First they demanded elections – they thought the others were going to win. And now, because the people have rejected them, they've provoked this war. While the sly Americans attack from the sea.'

'With what pretext?' asked Honório.

'They'll find one. Don't you worry. They're even capable of saying we started the war. Americans aren't afraid of sounding ridiculous . . .'

João Evangelista stepped aside for a short while from the dream that his life had become and recognized the person that was his wife. This was the victorious Carmina, the one he knew from old times. For the past two years she had toned down a bit. But now her eyes glistened, and it wasn't from the champagne. It was that same old glint, the one that had bewitched him once. Like all spells it was both fascinating and a little frightening. The phone rang and he went to answer – as a pretext to escape from those disturbing thoughts.

Carmina continued to make a most marvellous speech. Honório didn't dare to contradict her, even though it was quite obvious that he didn't entirely agree with her. But old habits linger; he had been moulded by the well-disciplined bureaucracy of a single-party system, and she was a member of the Central Committee and now a Parliamentarian, even though she had yet to take up her seat – and anyway nobody knew when Parliament would be sitting.

João returned to the lounge. He said, 'That was my father. He says everything's calm in his neighbourhood, but he's worried. Rumour has it that some of the Umbundu people are being persecuted by the locals. Some had to leave their houses and flee.'

'What did they expect?' said Carmina. 'Didn't the Umbundu vote for our enemies? Now they will suffer.'

'They didn't all vote that way,' said her husband. 'The results are there to prove it. And they are also part of the People – have you forgotten the old lessons? It's important to defend national unity: one People, one Nation.'

'They are Umbundu. They have ceased to be part of the People!'

'I am also Umbundu and I am part of the People.'

'Stop that, João. You are only Umbundu on your father's side. And what's more: you were born in Luanda. You are a Kimbundu on your mother's side. That means you are neither one nor the other. You are Angolan. You are National Unity. Our enemies call you Creole. They think it sounds offensive.'

'Very well, if I am National Unity then I have even more authority to speak. And I don't think we should persecute anyone – for any reason at all, much less for belonging to this or that ethnic group.'

'Didn't they persecute our people, be they Kimbundu or Umbundu or Muila or Kikongo?'

'I thought we were different,' said Margarida, who spoke for the first time. Then she seemed to take fright for having offended CAF by her rash remark.

João looked at her approvingly. He forgot all about his game. At that moment he had no desire to defeat the Russians, the

Americans or the Babylonians. He spoke very seriously to his wife:

'Admit that you've made a thoughtless remark, that it's not part of the ideology you subscribe to. You were letting off steam, that's all. And you should phone all your colleagues in the Central Committee and tell them to give orders to stop any persecutions. It is the only stand someone in a leadership position in our country should adopt, that is, if you want to deserve the respect and the legitimacy which the ballot box has given you.'

'We first need to know if it is true.'

'First we need to prevent it. Go on, telephone. Come on – you are a Member of Parliament. You are here to defend the people, all the people.'

It was almost as if it was meant to be: the radio began to broadcast appeals from the national police, and they were exactly about this: they warned that no persecution of civilians would be tolerated and that the authorities would punish any private settling of accounts. João sighed with relief.

'You see, Carmina? If the police are warning people not to do it, it's because someone's already done it. Fortunately, in the midst of all the madness of this stupid war, someone has had some good sense. It's a pity it wasn't you – it's a pity.'

He returned to his study while Carmina, contrite of heart, held on to the phone. And their friends returned to their tent in the middle of the square. More tents would be put up to house the homeless from the collapse of that fourth building. And in many other squares tents would be put up for all those who were fleeing from different parts of the country, for the war had now spread all over. And the havoc that had begun in Kinaxixi would spread to all the cities in a whirlwind of madness. Except that in other places the buildings didn't fall to musical accompaniment and without wounded victims, as they did in Kinaxixi. In other places the falling was red-coloured, bloodied.

◆

It was a soft and yet pained song that a child one day heard. She told her friends, and they scoffed at her: 'Since when does the water sing?'

'It's so pretty, but so sad,' repeated the child whose name was Cassandra. The building next to the lagoon, which is where Cassandra lived on the ninth floor, even had flats with brick walls. How those people had managed to carry bricks up those hazardous ladders was a mystery to all their neighbours. Voices were heard in protest: those refugees should be removed and they should finish constructing that building according to the proper regulations. The way it was to left to stand was a danger to everyone. Both to the people who lived there, as well as to the ones who lived in the square. But the illegal tenants paid little regard to these worries. Much rather live there than out on the street. And if the building came tumbling down with all of them inside nothing would happen to them: for weren't they in Kinaxixi Square where, when buildings collapsed, no one was left hurt? Cassandra persisted but her parents didn't wish to hear the song. Her friends laughed.

'Cassandra's really lost her marbles this time,' they said. 'Isn't a person who can hear what no one else can hear or who sees what's invisible to others mad?'

Yet the song rose up, more sorrowful still, from within the dark waters where the frogs and the river fish shared a home in the midst of the plants with the round leaves. Cassandra ceased to speak about this; it was pointless to do so. But she would often stand at the edge of the lagoon, listening attentively, her foot tapping to the music. And her girlish face would sadden like flowers at the end of the day.

◆

The days went by with news of other cities at war. Before then the war had occurred only in the interior; guerrilla activity had seemed close to them only because of the consequences it brought about. After the elections war became a city thing, a destroyer of buildings. The government tried to re-establish the army it had disbanded before the elections by recruiting its old military personnel in bulk, as well as by taking on new recruits. Hurriedly, it had to buy all the equipment which had been removed or sold for next to nothing. And one day Carmina arrived home whistling with excitement:

'You won't believe it! We've won the jackpot. Finally, we're rich. Yes, my darling, rich.'

João Evangelista made an effort to forget, at least for a few moments, about the war he was fighting against the Aztecs. He was Hernán Cortéz, about to conquer the fabled gold of the New World. It was probably time for lunch, and he got up without even looking at his watch.

'We're going to get rich in one fell swoop,' repeated his wife, already sitting at the table. 'Not in one, but in two fell swoops.'

'What's the deal?'

'Guns.'

Fortunately for João he was still serving himself. Had he been eating, he would have died choking. He stared at Carmina, his mouth wide open. She laughed, delighted that she had evoked such amazement in him. He was incapable of speaking; he just gaped, his mouth so wide it looked obscene.

'As you know, there's an international embargo against both sides in this conflict. That is to say, the legitimately elected government is not allowed to arm itself in defence against our enemies who have illegally kept all their military arsenal. But there's one way of resolving the question. Certain companies that have nothing to do with the government will buy arms and munitions on behalf of the government from companies in countries that don't even produce arms. Of course, the company that does this for the government will receive a commission, a small percentage because, after all, this is for a patriotic cause. Except that a small percentage in a business deal involving millions is thousands of dollars hundredfold. Dollars, not kuanzas or rubles or escudos. Dollars.'

'And your company . . .'

'Exactly. They contacted me, well – shit, man – since there's a deal to be made why shouldn't it be given to those comrades that have always remained steadfast? Why should we give it to others? All I have to do is send two faxes. That's all. Actually, I've already sent them. And in a few weeks' time there'll be hundreds of thousands of dollars in the bank account I opened in Sugaland – the new tax haven. As soon as this war ends we'll be off on holiday to Hawaii. If Joaquim Domingos, who's practically retarded, could go last year, why shouldn't we?'

Joaquim Domingos, the artillery officer, the one who destroyed shoals with his laser harpoon, was really an obsession with Carmina. Every time she made a deal, or was moving in on some line of business, she had to use that old friend whom she so bitterly criticized now as an example. Still, the reason for her criticism had changed with the times: now he was the one who was guilty of destroying the military arsenal for purely personal benefit. It occurred to João that one day he should try and work out the deeper reasons for this obsession. When he had time, that is, for he had more pressing worries.

'But Carmina, are you already in on this?'

'Of course, I've already sent the faxes. Now it's a matter of waiting for the goods. And there's an even bigger deal with the East. In a few weeks' time.'

'I'm not sure about this. With gun-running we're really getting into a big mess.'

'There's nothing messy at all. It's up to us to defend ourselves. And legally we're in the right. Didn't we win the elections which the UN declared to be free and just? So what's the problem? Do we have the right to defend ourselves, or don't we? The Americans made this embargo only so that the others would be able to take control by force. And there's already a lot of international pressure on the Americans to declare the embargo unfair.'

'I know that. But it's dirty money . . .'

'Drug-trafficking is dirty money. I'll never get involved with drugs, of course. This is different; this is clean and legitimate.'

Was it worth insisting? Carmina had made her mind up, and the pose she had adopted did not reveal a trace of guilt.

'If others can make use of the situation, then why shouldn't I, especially since it's a just cause? Convent morality's dead and gone. We're now living under a market economy, and there are three centuries of capitalist ethics to demonstrate how legitimate it all is.'

He didn't even respond; the harm had already been done and it was now shielded by the most convincing of arguments. All that is left – or so goes an old Lunda proverb – is for one to lower one's head like the crab and wait for the next wave. For it will come.

They finished their lunch and João returned to his computer. He had to show his face at work; it was days since he'd been there. With the war going on, things had got even more disorganized at work. They had even closed for two weeks because no one had gone to work. But his boss could well start becoming

48

demanding because in a time of confrontation bosses always became more tyrannical; it is as if they discover their military soul, and even the small-time director of a technically-bankrupt company can feel like a colonel in armoured combat. And he hated always having to remind them that he was married to a Member of Parliament and a member of the Central Committee who could make one hell of a noise should her husband be dismissed for absenteeism. He really had to show his face. But not this afternoon – well, it was too hot out on the street and Carmina had taken the car. He occupied himself with the sea routes to America, and after more than a few battles he was able to defeat the Aztecs. And then he moved north with all his ships and weapons with the intention of laying siege to the empire's stronghold. Thus another worry-free day went by, at the same time that Carmina was fighting to make herself rich. And how would things work out? Would both share in that sudden wealth or was it just for her? Vexed by his own doubts, he directed his rage against the arrogant Americans.

It was round about this time that they finalized the process of buying their flat, something which had taken them months. The State had freed itself of those dwellings which it had confiscated during the time of independence by selling them to their tenants. That is, only after the tenant had proved that he did not own real estate of any kind. That is why the flat went in João's name, for that would permit Carmina to buy the floor where her office was – at a later stage. But as influential as she was, the purchase of the flat was not done as quickly as they had wished for. However, now that the flat belonged to them, Carmina decided that it needed renovating. She hired a foreign building firm which sent a team headed by Mister Ribeiro, who was from the north of Portugal. It was necessary to take down walls and also close in the balcony at the back, change all the fittings in the bathroom, rewire the place, paint it. João didn't allow them to touch the study which was fine as it was. Only when everything else had been done would they give it a coat of paint.

The consequence was that, even with the air-conditioning on, there was still far too much background noise in the house, what with the hammer-beats and people talking, and furniture being constantly dragged from place to place. He tried to cope by raising the volume of his hi-fi set so as to drown the whirr of the air-conditioning, which in turn drowned the noises from the men at work. All this so that he could concentrate on his computer. Now and again Mister Ribeiro would come and ask something or inform him of something. Generally João would reply: 'That's up to my wife. She'll be home for lunch.'

He didn't want to waste time telling the men what to do; it was Carmina who was in charge at home, and he was quite all right with this. But there were times when he couldn't get rid of the foreman quickly enough. He had to listen to what he had to say: 'Because, doctor, you need to see this pipe we're going to change – it was rotten.' Or: 'Because, doctor, you really have to tell us whether the tap looks better on the side or in the middle 'cause if we wait for the Madam we'll waste a lot of time and you know how things are: our work has to be finished before the deadline because otherwise I'll be the one who gets the flak.'

At first João tried to explain that he wasn't 'doctor' – the title of someone who had graduated from university. 'But hang on, a person who's so intelligent, who spends the whole day working with that complicated machine they call a computer, such a person really deserves the title of doctor. I have a lot of respect for wisdom.' He couldn't very well say he didn't do a single thing, that he spent his entire day playing. Honesty was perfectly useless – because Mister Ribeiro would not believe him.

The Portuguese man was simple and very talkative; a friendly man. That's why João let him have his way sometimes. And one day, while they were in the kitchen, he opened the fridge and, in a gesture of intimacy, took out two beers. 'Something cold, Mister Ribeiro?'

'Doctor, forgive me but I should say no because if they found out at work I might get into trouble – and, never mind the war, I really do like this country and I don't want to be sent back to Portugal – but on the other hand it would be an offence against the good doctor. Oh yes, I'll accept it with much pleasure because this climate makes you so thirsty and it's as hot as hell – not as hell, as Africa.'

They drank their beers and with a bit of help from João the old man's tongue loosened.

'You know, doctor, I don't know what these people have in their veins. They heard a few shots and they all fled to the Motherland, and all building work stopped. Not me. I was shit scared for a few days; I'm not going to deny it and pretend I was the hero because I don't have to be one. I went back to work. I refused to be evacuated. The engineers, they were the first to go. You can't imagine how they were shitting their pants, they were almost shouting for their mommies, and they still haven't shown up at work. It seems as if some of them have been fired already because the war's finished and things have calmed down. Some other ones are handing in doctor's letters in order to stay there. And do you know what they say? That this is a war between blacks, that they were only here to earn some easy cash and to hell with the country. I tell you, doctor, engineers are the worst thing there is; they think they know a lot because they studied a few little sums and some little drawings, but they're as daft as my grandmother – God protect her – who is actually a good woman. Well, I listened to them at the office. Always saying bad things. Now that it's almost as if they're not here, the work is easier to get done. And they carry on speaking ill of these people who received them so well. If

51

anyone asks them about Angola they all say: It's a horde of savages who will kill each other for a morsel of bread, which is not true, because Angolans are people like us and I haven't met an engineer who is as educated as you, doctor, if you will forgive the comparison. I have been here for three years and I have no cause to complain. I don't agree with what they say in my country about all this. You know what they say on television, don't you? That they're killing off all the people who are not from here. I swear I've never seen that. In the group of workers that I work with there are people from all sides.'

'You're very well informed about the kind of things people say in Portugal, Mister Ribeiro. How do manage to find all this out?'

'Don't I have family and friends there? They phone me to ask what's going on and sometimes I read the papers that arrive. Not much though – they make me want to puke. I bet you most journalists are either engineers or people who tried to study to become engineers.'

'Mister Ribeiro, I see you don't like engineers. You know, I actually studied engineering, but I gave it up.'

'Just as well you did, doctor. You deserve all respect for having given it up. It is proof that you are a good person.'

Things with Carmina were not so good. She would come home for lunch, which was often late because of the disorder in the kitchen where they were taking a wall down, unjustly reprimand Joana, the maid, and then she would go and discover some little aspect of the renovations that did not please her. Mister Ribeiro did his best to defend his company. But the arguments were never-ending. He didn't complain to João; he always said, 'The client is always right', but he would always leave dangling a few observations like: Was it really necessary for the bathroom floor to be pink? Why couldn't it be blue or white, the colours they had? Given the circumstances at the time, certain demands seemed somewhat excessive because goods were just not available. Everything had to be imported, and this was a lengthy process. Carmina didn't want to know about this. She paid and therefore her wishes had to be satisfied. For João some of these were no more than silly whims, but he wouldn't get involved; he had promised this to himself right from the start. Mister Ribeiro lowered his head; he tried to appease her.

'Let's do as the lady wants,' he would say to João, 'but I know what's going to happen: I'll be in for a hiding from the engineer; that's all he knows how to do.'

'By the way, doctor, there's something I don't understand. I'm sorry for sounding so cheeky – I know you won't take offence, you're an understanding person. Your domestic tells me her name's not Joana, but Fátima. They call her Fatita at home, which I think sounds much nicer than Joana. Why do you call her that?'

Joana looked at the Portuguese man in fright and fled from the kitchen. João smiled, without knowing quite why he was doing it; he was somewhat embarrassed, for the question touched a sore spot. He shouldn't act offended and his answer should give no indication that he was offended, especially since the other man had clearly not meant to be malicious, but was being his usual naïve self.

'Mister Ribeiro, it's a little quirk of my wife's. We have had many different maids. They don't seem to stay. This one seems to have lasted longer. That's why my wife decided that she didn't have the patience to learn a new name every time. The first one was called Joana, so all the other ones got to be called Joana.'

'Strange, isn't it?' was Mister Ribeiro's only comment.

João took refuge in his study. He was bothered by the question which reminded him of an old bone of contention he'd had with Carmina. It was the colonial madams who changed the names of their domestics to Maria or Joana – there's evidence of this in literature. His wife had taken her lessons from those colonial madams and, even after Independence, she continued to play by the same rules. When he pointed this out to her they had a tough argument, but as always CAF won the day. And even the domestics always ended up accepting it. Deep down, what did it matter if they changed their names? What was important for them was to keep their jobs. In those days, when the struggle was for the eradication of social classes, this could have been interpreted as a symptom of tyranny and élitism, and a politician would have come toppling down from his pedestal if this had reached the ears of the trade unions. But not even this argument dissuaded Carmina: 'The Party has no reason to poke its nose into my house.'

He quite agreed with this, although he didn't think it prudent to air this too publicly. Strange Carmina with her contradictions. As strange as that grudge she bore against that artillery officer, Joaquim Domingos. Nicely hidden secrets. He shrugged his shoulders and opted to play the game.

Chapter Four

The war, even though it was taking place far from Luanda, set the rhythm of life for people. Conversations were always introduced with this subject – even though other topics of conversation would crop up later, such as the usual scandal-mongering about the wife who was cheating on her husband, or the one topic that until then had been the most interesting thing to talk about: business. Business was obviously prospering very slowly on account of the shortage of money as a result of the new outbreak of war. That is, except for the buying of arms and military equipment, but that was a topic reserved for few of the elect.

Carmina was now an habitué of the luxurious boutiques that existed side by side with the indescribable misery of refugees and of children who had been orphaned or abandoned and who filled the streets of the capital, and who slept without shelter next to the porticos of the boulevard along the seacoast, or on the sand of the Island of Luanda. CAF said that now that she had money she could afford the luxury of dressing well; long gone and forgotten was the austerity of the Youth activist. Parliament was opened, but without the bulk of the members of the rebel party which had since taken up arms. She spent most of her day on the benches of the majority party, which did not prevent her from taking care of her business deals which, by the way, never took up too much of her time. The only time she felt a little under pressure was when she had to deal with the import of three containers of whisky crates at the same time as there was an important debate in the Assembly. She asked João to take care of a certain piece of paper since he was planning to leave the house that day to go to work.

'It's dead easy. You won't waste much time at the bank. Everything's been arranged already. You see, if I send Francisca then nothing will get sorted out.' Francisca was her secretary, the only staff member in her company. Her main duties were to answer the phone and take care of the faxes.

João really had to go to work. He muttered to himself: 'I have finally started my career in the company as a message-boy.' He agreed to do it, as he agreed to any request made by his wife. Actually, he didn't waste more than five minutes on that piece of paper. Was everything that easy, after all? He had a horror of bureaucracy, because of the sort of person he was, and he had imagined an entire morning wasted at the bank. He left with the paper, much relieved, and even reconciled to Carmina's business activities.

The problems began when Carmina arrived home for lunch. She was livid. She immediately lambasted Joana, alias Fatita, discovered that everything the stonemasons had done was wrong, and because Mister Ribeiro was already gone by then and she couldn't take out her rage on him, it had to be João who listened to her as she unburdened herself.

'Can you imagine it, those hypocrites want to pass a law that will forbid Members of Parliament from being company directors. They say it's incompatible. Ah, they're going to hear it good and proper. A bunch of incompetent idiots who want to be professional politicians, and live off a miserable Member of Parliament's salary? Do these half-baked Franciscans want to nurture misery as though it's a virtue? As if this would make the people think better of them. The people only respect the rich and powerful. Haven't they got it yet?'

56

'You were a professional politician for many years and it was all fine by you. It was Lenin's thesis, have you forgotten?'

CAF cast him a fiery glance. João shrunk into his chair; he regretted having spoken.

'It was a different context and the objectives were different. This is a market economy now. How are they going to have businessmen represented in Parliament? How are they going to open the party to all the social classes, if they force them to give up their businesses?'

'They won't give up their businesses. They'll put up some straw men who'll officially own the companies, but they'll continue to run them. That's the way they do it in democratic countries.'

'I know that. And that's what they are going to force us to do. Hypocrites! Half a dozen of us opposed them. But we were defeated at the outset by the mass of populists who want to give Parliament some prestige by making out that Members of Parliament represent anonymous and pitiful people.'

'But don't they?'

'Bullshit! It's just hypocrisy.'

'But have they already approved the law?'

'Not yet. The document's very big. But this clause has already gone through and there's nothing we can do about it. The principle of it has already been accepted.'

João Evangelista didn't ask any more. It wasn't the sort of talk that pleased him. Instinctively. Whichever way it turned out, there would always be something left over for him.

He didn't go to work that afternoon. He had already fulfilled his weekly obligation by going that morning. The salary he received didn't justify greater sacrifices. He went to the study in order to destroy more enemy cities, thereby perfecting the infallible strategy that would give him a world empire and, when the game ended, would earn him the title of 'Conqueror'. Under him would be a gallery of portraits of leaders that he had defeated, and these ranged from Alexander the Great and Rameses to Stalin and Mao. But for the entire afternoon he was haunted by the presage of something terrible.

A presage which was confirmed when, on arriving home that evening, Carmina invited him to dinner at the most expensive restaurant in Luanda. 'I know exactly what's going to happen and no good's coming out of it.' But how could he not take up such a warm-hearted invitation from the adorable Carmina who was on top form once again?

Was it the repetition of something that had already happened or was it merely his intuition that made him the see the entire scene as having taken place already? The restaurant was in fact very good, the staff most courteous, and the food first class. CAF spoke about things to do with Parliament: what so-and-so had said to defend such a point, and how such-and-such had replied to a perfidious accusation from a member of the opposition. And also how some shipment or other of silk and brocade which she had ordered for one of the high-class boutiques was about to arrive.

He was about to say, 'But Carmina, you should think of food because people are dying of hunger,' but he stopped at the exact moment that he opened his mouth. Annoying her just wasn't worth it. The worst was still to come. He even knew when the moment would come: when they were sipping their after-dinner drinks. The film was running with all the grain that came from its already having been reeled and screened. Nothing was unpredictable. His wife also informed him that they were going to buy a new car. The old one she had inherited from the Y was falling apart, and there were some very comfortable recent models. They had left behind the Communist misery of the past.

She was still waiting for the cars for the Members of Parliament, but only a few would get distributed, and the members of the opposition would get priority. 'Poor things, they're so hard up. That way they'll be more willing to co-operate with the majority party.'

João knew she hadn't invited him out to give him the news about a new car; the topic just wasn't worth the cost of dinner. That's why he limited himself to asking what make she'd chosen.

'A Japanese one, of course – to spite our American friends.' Her hatred for the empire had not subsided. She was consistent about this, as she was about many other things. Finally the cognacs came. Her eyes were smiling brightly when she asked him:

'You do remember our conversation at lunch?'

'We have arrived,' he thought, resigned to the consequences. He leaned back on his chair. The time had come to have his own back at the resentment of being the wounded male. He nodded his head.

'That law's really going to go through. I was speaking to those of my colleagues who are both Members of Parliament and businessmen. And as always, your brilliant idea will be adopted by all of us. It is our only alternative.'

'My idea?' His defensive strategies had been well planned, but she had succeeded in catching him by surprise.

'Of course. Your brilliant idea. My darling, it's odd how it's only you that doesn't recognize his own intelligence. Wasn't it you who said that what was necessary was to hand over the nominal ownership of the companies to people whom we have absolute trust in? We have come to celebrate our new corporation. We are partners now. You are the boss. And they can approve the Incompatibility Law for all I care.'

Now that you need me, you invite me to become a partner. I

never wanted to be part of such a corporation, but I hoped you had invited me out of courtesy so that I could have had the pleasure of saying no.

'When I formed the company I wanted you to be involved. But I knew what your answer would be. That you weren't born for business, that you hated bureaucracy and that you would have to fight against that. That's why I spared you. I took responsibility for everything, because all I wished for was to leave you calm and happy in your little corner with your books and your computer. But I am at the crossroads and that's why I am asking you to help. I don't trust anyone else. I know you're thinking this will give you a lot of work. I promise I'll take care of everything. The only necessary formality is for us to go the public notary to sign a new deed that will have both our names as partners. It's obvious you'll have to sign a few papers now and then. You don't even have to read them. I'll take care of all that. That's all I am asking you for. Please.'

He had seen the film before, except that, as always happens with repeats, the tone was not what he had come to expect. A comma had changed place in the sentence, and that had changed the nature of the speech. There could be no doubt that Carmina was a daughter of her party.

'All right, you take care of everything. But you decided to get involved, in arms deals for example, and the one who'll get the flak will be me.'

'There you go again with that story. Everything was perfectly legal. No one can accuse us of anything. I promise you I won't take any decision that will place you in a dicey situation. And you can keep your job because the question of incompatibility doesn't apply to you.'

Carmina was begging with her eyes. It was the same thing she had done when she wanted to marry him and he was reluctant to do so. He liked her, he wanted to live with her, even die with her, but marriage seemed like a heavy burden, for they were both young. And there was Mateus Evangelista's avowed opposition. That's why he hesitated. She looked at him in a certain manner – underneath it all she was a defenceless little girl, despite the veneer of strength and confidence. He had yielded to it, and was ready to face the wrath of his parents.

He had never known how to say no to such a passionate plea. His wounded pride had dissolved in the air with the explanation she had given: she hadn't made him a partner in order to spare him; it wasn't to offend or belittle him. And he believed her. Because João faithfully believed in Carmina's love. She had never given him any reason to doubt it. There was only one thing which had intrigued him of late.

'Let's put our cards on the table. We're changing the topic, but it's still connected . . . What happened between you and Joaquim Domingos?'

The astonishment stamped on her face was genuine. It remained like that for a few seconds. But soon her eyes were smiling, glinting. And after that came a grimace bred out of rage.

'That scoundrel! It's amazing – how did you find out? I never told you because it didn't concern you. It would just irritate you and that wouldn't help. But since you think it's important . . . Some time after we got married – a year later, I think – Joaquim Domingos started chasing me. He made a few suggestions. Obviously I gave him a flat "No". He was furious. He threatened to ruin me politically. He said I would never rise in the Y – he was an old activist and he wielded a lot of influence. Of course, I rose up in the Y and in the Party, and he's corrupt to the core. That's it. Why tell you? Would it have helped with anything? Just like I didn't tell you about the others who ogle me with their eager eyes. Except that this one went too far. He abused his power. He actually threatened me.'

61

The truth. That was true. João didn't doubt it even for a second. Why not trust her completely? There was a pause: a road forked somewhere along the main road, and once again he faced a tremendous problem. He had to decide. It was a lot easier if he were a Zulu and wanted to create a world empire – he had either to choose between the western option (invade America) or the northern option (invade Europe). But this wasn't a game; this was about real life.

'I'll make one pre-condition if I am to accept being a partner-boss – the one who can very well land up in jail if something goes wrong.'

'Don't be melodramatic. This is a clean business. Everything's above board. But I accept your pre-condition, my darling – even without knowing what it is, because I know it will be reasonable.'

'That there should be no business involving guns and munitions. Buy uniforms for the soldiers, food for the soldiers, rucksacks, all fine, but guns and munitions, no.'

'I had anticipated your request and I had already agreed to it. I'll abide by your condition.'

Carmina called a waiter and ordered a bottle of champagne, the most expensive of the French ones – because that's the way things are done in Luanda: we go hungry but we have the best French champagne and the oldest whisky. Many die after drinking cheap spirits illegally distilled with batteries to accelerate the process of fermentation, but those don't count: they are the ones who have been marginalized by the process, by this political system and the previous one. After they had amorously clinked their glasses and taken the first sip, she said:

'We won a million dollars with the arms deal, and it's already earning interest in Sugaland. With your pre-condition, my darling, we have just lost more than three million. Everything was ready. All that needed to be done was to send the usual faxes.

But that's quite all right. Tomorrow I'll hand the matter over to Rodrigo, who's one of the businessmen I can trust and who needs a little support now that his wife's left him for a Senegalese man.'

She said this with a certain levity, without any hint of recrimination. They finished their glasses and re-filled them. In grand style. They wouldn't be leaving the place until they had finished the bottle. They could leave a little bit for the waiter to wet his lips with. They left for their house, whispering promises of love-making that night.

As they drove up towards Kinaxixi, they saw that the building which had stood on the right edge of the square was lying on the ground. Hundreds of people were searching in the rubble. The police had cordoned off the road and they had to drive along the left. The tricolor of some European country which used to fly high up a building must have gently flown towards the ground because now it was fluttering in the hands of children, as though this were a political march, or the victorious final of some basketball Africa Cup. The confusion at large in the square seemed to have become worse. The place looked like some festival with tents. There was also water on the tarmac, and that was something new. Some pipe must have burst. Driving on the left side of the square, João noticed that the water seemed to come from higher up, not from the building which had just fallen down.

◆

Cassandra heard the song that was beckoning her. She moved closer to the lagoon that was forming itself next to the building under construction. It was night already, and there were still cars in Kinaxixi, but nothing like the dense traffic of daytime; it was all much slower now because of all the accumulated rubble.

It was a full moon, but one could see it only by looking directly at the moon because the illumination towers in the square made its brightness less evident. The song was much stronger than usual. If only she could understand a word or two. Cassandra, who was born in Luanda, could understand only Portuguese. To her it seemed she could hear words in that language. Did the Water Spirit – for that was how she referred to the voice that sang the sorrowful song – wish to speak to her? She went to wake up Janico, who was already sleeping. They climbed down the building very carefully; he moaning and groaning with sleep: 'I'm so sick of your crazy idea about the Water Spirit. You're losing it.'

The song was becoming louder still and the level of the dark water was rising. Some of the water was overflowing on to the pavement. They tried to listen. In the midst of all those incomprehensible sounds she could make out words she knew, but Janico shook his head: his sister was doing her 'pracs' – practising how to be mad – as they now called it. But one thing was certain – the water was running down the pavement, dragging with it some of the leaves from the round waterplants that had grown on the surface of the lagoon and had fed the river fish and the toads. Cassandra didn't want to go back to the building under construction, for she could not sleep; she was drawn by the soft sorrowful song, fascinated by the sheet of water that ran down the sides, but he pulled her away, almost pushed her towards the improvised ladder and they climbed up to their little compartment.

◆

The muddy dark water that had escaped from the small lagoon next to the building under construction was going to be the motive for much gossip, much research and many reports.

Municipal workers excavated the area above the lagoon looking for a pipe that was possibly rotting and adding to the volume of the water arising from next to the unfinished building. They didn't find anything. The water system seemed normal. Of course, for the waterworks company, a system was regarded as normal so long as the water didn't spout excessively from all pipes and holes; normality is also a relative thing. But the water continued to spurt out on to the pavement; it ran across Kinaxixi Square, and down Rua da Missão – Mission Street. That made the traffic flow difficult, for it had to be redirected to the right in the direction of the Marginal, the road alongside the seacoast boulevard. The water carved holes in the tarmac. The drains which had been created to take away the rainwater would still function for a few days. But then they clogged up and the seacoast boulevard began to get flooded over – because of the inability of the authorities to take the necessary steps and much to the anger of drivers. Letters to the press demanded that measures be taken. Ordinary people interviewed for TV said enough was enough and that something had to be done. On the radio they used the opportunity to poke fun at some of the initiatives but also made a call demanding urgent action. But what, considering they knew so little? The brook was looking for its old riverbed and wanted to discharge into the bay. The boulevard along the seacoast prevented it from doing so.

A columnist suggested that they should dig an exit to the sea. But another columnist complained that for that they would need suction pumps, dredges, heaven knows what. Arnaldo Santos, the writer from Kinaxixi, smiled and said that what they needed to do was to close the Rua da Missão exit and put all the rubble from the fallen building in one place, just as the Carmelite fathers had done a few centuries back with sand. This would allow Kinaxixi lagoon to be reconstituted, for such was the desire of Kianda the Water Spirit. His wife thought he was

65

raving mad: 'Don't talk about that in public because if you do so we'll be ridiculed.' But whenever people began talking about the water which was always spouting out from the small lagoon caught between the buildings, he would repeat his idea in a voice that was so mysterious that his listeners weren't sure whether he was speaking or he was prophesying. And like some marvel the water was carving out its own riverbed, and as it went along it left a crack in the land.

At long last there was something to replace the international press's image of Angola as a nation at war. When the great papers or TV stations spoke of the country, it was to explain the evolution of the Luanda Syndrome. The Pope prayed for peace, but also that the cause of the Syndrome would be discovered. Because in the mind of everyone the two apparently different phenomena were connected: the fact of the buildings tumbling down to the accompaniment of tinkling sounds, and bloodlessly at that, and the water which sprouted from nothing at all – this in a place that was almost barren.

A well-known American seismologist arrived on the scene with a theory which he had concocted long before he had arrived and before the first mosquito had bitten his rounded butt. On his arrival at the airport, and in the presence of the multitude of journalists who were there to greet him, he declared that Luanda was in a seismically active region and that he had come to study the intensity of the quakes because it was clear, self-evident in fact – only the blind could not see it – that the two phenomena were caused by the same thing: the tremors and the possibly fatal fissures that were being produced inside the Earth's crust.

Because there was no living memory of an earthquake in the Luanda region, or even of something like a hiccough in the land, the journalists were stunned and proclaimed to the world that what was happening in Luanda was the same as had happened in the San Andreas fault in California. This was proved by the real rift that the water gushing from the Kinaxixi had created all along Rua da Missão and the seacoast boulevard.

Master Mingo, renowned city thief, let this be known to his accomplices: 'Brothers, this old man is cool. He's saying Luanda's like Los Angeles. Yeah, we've got to get more professional. We need to assault banks, kidnap the rich. What's this, stealing cars? That's outdated. We've got to copy the Yankees in the way we do things.'

The war continued unabated, but people forgot about it unless they were directly involved; they were enticed by the more recent phenomena. The French were more generous still. Instead of a seismologist, they sent a team of specialists, a huge inter-disciplinary team headed by a well-known spy. It even included an expert in volcanology.

In the bars many Luandaners laughed about this: 'Next they're going to say this is a volcano that doesn't spit fire but water that's as dirty as a river fish.' A charter plane full of German tourists then arrived, immediately followed by one with South Africans, then one with Japanese, and then, surprising as it sounds, with Finns. They came with their anti-mosquito repellents, their travel bags with medication against snake and scorpion bites, electronic credit cards which were not accepted because the habit had not yet caught on, photographic cameras, video cameras, tape recorders, machines to measure arterial tension and to feel the pulse, tinned food, white pith hats and khaki shorts, introductory letters and the usual sort of things tourists bring when they visit a country of savages.

A Japanese man whom the Luandaners immediately named 'Goatee' on account of his small beard, set up his camper's tent in the middle of the square, next to the tents of the refugees. Armed with all his oriental patience, he would stand for days behind his camera mounted on a tripod. It was focused on the few buildings which remained standing on the side of the square where the first building had fallen. Crew members from the Angolan TV network derided the efforts of the Japanese man. They chatted him up, filmed him and made programmes on this odd cameraman who had made a bet he could film a building falling down. He had even set his sights on the exact building because for twenty-four hours his video camera was focused on the same building. The TV crew jeered and then went off to some rave or other. A typical mistake of the under-developed. When the restaurant building fell, only Goatee was there to film the whole scene. It was the first time you could watch a video recording of a Kinaxixi building falling down, and in slow motion if you so desired. Goatee sold his video to an American TV network that is watched all over the world, got rich on the proceeds, and went on to build an anti-seismic house on some Japanese island. And the Angolan TV crew ate their hearts out: the blasted Jap had taught them how patience really did pay off.

'Jeez, man, we had something right under our noses, and we let the Japanese walk away with it.' Only a lot of beer could make them forget how very frustrated they felt.

With Goatee's video it was now possible to study the phenomenon a bit better. And to observe the reactions of the Spanish lady who, caught in mid-air between contrary winds, had only one concern on her mind: and that was to wrap her skirt tightly around her body so no one would see her panties. Or the child who smiled and flapped his arms as he tried to fly. Or the doctor who came down holding his stethoscope. Or the policeman holding up his pants because he was on the toilet seat. Still, different schools of thought clashed over interpretation; specialists from the various fields fought each other with fists and sometimes with their feet, as they do in certain respectable Parliaments; and no one was able to present a plausible hypothesis that would explain the causes of the Luanda Syndrome. Even with the Japanese man's video.

The only ones who were pleased with the vagueness of the studies were the owners of hotels, restaurants and snack bars. As long as the phenomenon remained a mystery, the number of tourists grew. At last, Luanda had become an attractive place for those who liked strong emotions – other than from the war, that is. Because the war brought clients, too: the cannon sellers, the bankrupt businessmen who came looking for strange deals, the journalists. The crooks were also happy; they had even invented a song:

> Let all the buildings fall
> one by one
> slowly
> so the dollars will reach
> our hands trembling
> like the buildings falling down.

The street kids also got a few more hand-outs and for them it made little difference if the buildings fell since they had no homes anyway. Let them fall, let them fall, the whole lot, one by one, slowly . . .

◆

The song she could hear from the edge of the lagoon was similar to the other one. What she began to pick out were more than random words. 'Let them fall, one by one, slowly.' Then words. And a phrase which she understood only because she heard it on the lips of the Kinaxixi writer who was taking a walk through the rubble of the square: 'Kianda's wish.' It wasn't enough to understand the meaning of the message. But the song was becoming stronger and stronger and, almost imperceptibly, it was getting less and less sorrowful; slowly, bit-by-bit, it was transforming itself into a battle song. Why was she the only one who heard it? Why couldn't Janico hear it? Tapping out the beat, she would become sad, but at the same time she felt drawn by that dark water. It was as if something from deep under the water were beckoning her. Her heart closed in a knot as it whispered its own sadness.

Chapter Five

The renovation work at home was almost finished. It was only after he had seen the Japanese man's video and the commentaries about it on TV that it occurred to João Evangelista that Carmina's idea was quite absurd – it was like some sort of indefinable old feeling that had long hovered over him, but which, because of his distractedness, he had not grasped at first. It was only now, with the construction work at an end, that what was obvious dawned on him all the more clearly. But he was generous by nature and avoided blaming his wife. He took responsibility for some of the blame. Naturally. That's how he had been raised.

'We've made one hell of a mistake. Doing renovations in a building that's about to fall down.'

Carmina looked at him very seriously. She was silent, as if digesting the words. It took some time before she said anything; she spoke in a thin voice:

'Do you really think it's about to fall, João? We're not in the square.'

'We're behind the buildings in the square. What guarantee do we have that the phenomenon won't come all the way here and start demolishing the adjacent buildings? You always wanted a real house and we've wasted all this money for nothing in this flat. Much better to buy a house quite a distance from this place. We've got the cash for it. It's obvious, Carmina. Why did I only think of it now?'

'I never considered it . . . But actually, what guarantee do we have? I've always heard them referring to the Kinaxixi buildings. The Kinaxixi ones . . . Since this is already in Rua do Cónego I didn't even think of it. You're right, we've got to buy a house outside this area. Urgently. Business is doing well. We can afford to invest in that.'

'There are still three buildings to go – if there's any logic to any of this.'

As a matter of fact, there were still three buildings standing: the one under construction, the one that faced it on the other side of Avenida dos Combatentes and the one with the market. The others were now reduced to heaps of rubble. After those three had fallen anything could happen. And why should those three fall first? João avoided thinking about this by playing with greater fury; he invented new strategies to establish his empire more quickly, much more quickly; he defeated all the other civilizations, and this gave him better scores.

In the meantime Carmina was looking for a house. Her old idea was to have a house built in the southern part of the city, beyond Funtungo de Belas, on a hill from where they could gaze at Mussulo Bay. There was talk about creating South Luanda – in effect, a city for the rich. With condos surrounded by lawns, swimming pools and a well organized security system. But that would take years and there was a certain urgency now. The problem was that those who owned houses preferred to rent them out to foreigners or to organizations, get the rent in dollars, and live comfortably off the rent money. The houses that were for sale were either too small or in unsatisfactory locations. The only time a good house came on the market was when someone decided to leave the country for good, and that didn't happen often; those sort of houses were owned by foreign companies. Carmina was getting more and more nervous as time moved on. Every day she spoke of the imminent catastrophe. She referred to it as *The Thing* that had occurred in Kinaxixi. She no longer attributed it to sabotage.

Another kind of complication blew up when Carmina arrived at the flat at a time different than usual and found Mister Ribeiro and Joana, alias Fatita, lost in a rapturous kiss in her kitchen. João left his computer as soon as he heard his wife's screams; he came running to find out what disaster had occurred. The Portuguese man blushed; he apologized – would the good doctor help him out because they were quite serious about all this. They liked each other very much. He had promised to marry her. Everything legal. This was no game.

But Carmina would have none of this; she had already fired Joana and to him she was saying: 'Go back to your company. I don't want to see you ever again in my house. They can send me somebody else to finish the work. I'm going to pack you off on the first plane heading for your country. I'm going to raise one hell of a scandal. You'll see. I will not tolerate such lack of respect in my kitchen. You don't let my maid work. That explains why recently lunch has always been served late. All you do is upset things. And what's worse, everything you've done is sloppy. One hell of a sum I've wasted on all this, and when the building comes down that money will have practically gone up in smoke.'

João tried to pour oil over troubled water. 'Patience, patience. Let's talk about it. It's not as if it's the end of the world. They're not minors, and they've already been vaccinated.'

But Carmina wouldn't have any of it: 'That thing over there, out of my house! Don't ever set foot here ever again. And you, Mister, take your men now. I want another team to finish the work. To hell with your company.' Which would put Mister Ribeiro in a neat pickle. His boss would never forgive him for the scandal, and in the home of a Parliamentarian at that. That would be the end of any company. He was in disgrace, fired from work, sent away from Angola on the first plane in accordance with the 20/24 Procedure, that is to say, twenty kilos of luggage and twenty-four hours to leave the country.

'Only you, good doctor, can save me. Convince your wife that the intentions weren't bad. It's love. It's a fickle beast that catches hold of us when we least expect it.'

Carmina frothed at the mouth: 'Damned white man, you think because this is a black people's home that you can do anything.'

And it was that remark that made João Evangelista scream at his wife for the first time: 'Shut your trap. Now you come out with cheap racism. I will not tolerate that. It could have happened to any of us.' The 'Shut your trap' was so strong, so cutting, that CAF was left totally speechless. Never before had he dared to speak like this. But she lowered her head, didn't answer back; perhaps it was because he had shouted at her for the first time in her life, or perhaps it was because she accepted that she was wrong, for it is true that she had spent her entire youth shouting, 'Down with Racism', and now it rose to the surface at the first opportunity, which is why she took refuge in her room, leaving João to sort out the mess.

'You must calm down, Mister Ribeiro. You have to admit that it showed a lack of respect. I'm not interested in what you do outside. You can't do it inside the house.'

'You are quite right about that. I see the error of my ways.'

But Fatita was smiling at him and it was obvious they did meet outside the house. They really did want to tie the knot. She was smiling, smiling that wily smile, and he had an irresistible urge to kiss her: 'I was a fool. Forgive me. Don't let me fall in disgrace. I don't want to leave this blessed land. And what will happen to me if I lose my job?'

And João said: 'Don't fret. We're not going to make a

74

complaint. I'll see to my wife. But you'd better finish the work right now because I don't know what will happen if my wife catches you in the house again.'

'The work's done, doctor. I was only making a last inspection. The civil engineer might be coming here tomorrow to check everything.'

'Then I suggest he come when my wife's not here because she might just tell him what happened. As for you, Joana, or rather, Fatita, I very much doubt it if Madam will accept you again. I don't know.'

'I'll take care of her, doctor. We'll be together sooner than we thought. After all, it's better like that. But I have to thank you once again. You saved my life. There are few people like you. That's what I say, Sir.'

The two left and João could make out the Portuguese man saying to Joana: 'That's a real gentleman. He's a real cool guy. He should be a government minister in my country.' He smiled and went to face Carmina who had taken refuge in the bedroom.

Much to his surprise, he found her calm and collected. She was composing herself in front of the mirror of the dressing table. She spoke quite naturally:

'How did the scene end?'

'The work's finished. You don't need to see him ever again. Joana, too. She's gone already. Case closed. And there's no complaint to the company, otherwise they'll screw him good and proper. They're going to live together and produce a lot of little mulattoes. At the rate it's going I'll be the godfather to one of them.'

'You must admit it was . . .'

'You must admit you really put your foot in it. Black or white, what does it matter?'

'I know. It slipped out.'

And that was because the idea was lodged deep down in her

brain. Such a thing would never slip out of his lips, thought João Evangelista. But he let the case rest. Carmina had experienced too many strong emotions for one day. He had to spare her. She was under stress with the idea of flying down with the building and with the war and with the country torn to pieces. He immersed himself in the game and barely noticed it when she came to the study to say goodbye.

She left and not long afterwards the building fell. The one directly opposite the unfinished building. He went over to the window to see what had happened. He could see the rubble from the new downfall through the space left open by the former Cuca Beer building. Two to go, he counted. Which one would be next? The one with the market or the other one? *We accept bets.* It had only just occurred to him now, but surely there was already some sort of large-scale lottery in the city with predictions about the next fall. People wouldn't let an opportunity like that go by. And that was when he remembered Honório, homeless and now jobless, and probably wifeless, too.

The evening before his friend had come to ask him if he had been to the company. No, he had to go there some time this week.

'You don't know what's happened to me. I'll tell you now, because you'll find out about it when you go there. I was kicked out. And I have to admit that they were in the right.'

That wasn't possible. They fired him and he agreed with it. João forgot the moves of the game that he would be making next, and this was something that hardly ever happened to him. Normally when he spoke to someone he only heard half of what they said; the other half of his brain was busy with the game that he had been obliged to abandon temporarily. This time he was all attention.

'You know, I have to get money for a house. To buy bricks and cement, to pay for the workers. I've managed to get a bit of land. It's impossible to build even a room with the salary we get. Of course, you don't have those kinds of problems. You're lucky you're married to Carmina, but this is everyone else's fate. Ninety-nine per cent of the population. I had to get by. You follow?'

João understood perfectly and he nodded in agreement. So much beating about the bush. This was something serious. Again he was apprehensive about what had happened to his friend. He limited himself to listening.

'How's a minor clerk like me going to find an extra source of income? If I had a company car, I'd use it as a taxi. It would be like rounding off the figures of the salary. If I was in a government department, I'd ask for a fee to issue a particular certificate or testimonial. If I was a teacher, I'd sell the exams to the students. Isn't that what they do? But what can we do in our company? I worked with figures, with accounts. All this abstract stuff. Then I remembered. The only thing I could do was to make a deal with the people who owed money to the company. I'd reduce their debt figure and they'd pay me a small commission. Bad luck! I was only able to make one good deal. It didn't give me much. A few million kuanza. At least it was a bit more than a month's salary. When I tried to do it a second time I was caught. It's just bad luck because by some crazy coincidence my boss asked me for the files of that client whose figures I had falsified. There were still some documents with the real figures. I hadn't had time to change everything. He saw the fraud. Well, OK, the boss didn't want a scandal. He gave me a resignation letter to sign right there and then. The other alternative was to go to the police. Of course, I signed. What else could I do?'

'You'd be the first to be jailed for corruption.'

'Right. And it got worse when I told Margarida. I had to tell her. She's as livid as a snake. She won't talk to me. Says she never thought her husband was as corrupt as the others. Does it help to say it's only petty corruption, that it's nothing like the massive corruption that's bringing down our country? For her it's all the same: corruption is corruption. She's gone to her uncle's house. She wants a divorce.'

'You've lost your wife, as well?'

'Everything. Home, job, wife. All because of this Luanda Syndrome or whatever it is.'

João had no words with which to console his friend. He handed him a bottle of whisky. At least it helped him to forget. He looked at his friend drinking glass after glass; neither of them spoke. The poor are so poor that even when they steal they are poor at it – they get caught in no time. Would it help to reveal these thoughts of his to Honório? Yet, despite the fact that this was a much bandied about saying, it was the only thing that came to mind. Honório had always been an example to others. During those days when there were Red Saturdays he would be the first to volunteer to work. He was the first to join the company's People's Defence Organization, and he had received praise for catching a thief who was trying to steal company goods. Converted to the new philosophy as a result of the political changes, he preached democracy and tolerance. Always faithful to the same political party, Carmina's. Thrust into a life of crime – if we can call it that – because salaries are swallowed up by inflation; they're not even enough to buy a week's groceries. And what's worse, he had to find a place to live. What would he have done under those circumstances? He had studied much more than Honório, and perhaps he would be a bit more cautious, a bit more astute; he would devise a better method of increasing his salary. But shit, deep down he would be doing the same thing.

'Look, I'm going to talk to Carmina. I'll only tell her the basics. That you're out of a job. I'm sure she'll find you a better one.'

By now half-drunk, Honório burst out sobbing. He moaned, 'What am I reduced to? My God, what am I reduced to?'

João couldn't make out if what he was referring to was the fact that he didn't have a home, or that he was jobless, or that he'd lost his wife, or that he needed Carmina to help him find a job.

'My man. I promise you I'll even talk to her today. She'll find you something. She knows everyone. She's very influential.'

That night Carmina did promise to find a solution. It would be in a friend's company. So he could be paid in dollars. 'Honestly, he can't survive with the ridiculous salaries they pay.'

João had to remind her again today. Every day, until she did what she had promised to do. And he had no reason to feel guilty about it. He was sure that with a new job and a decent salary, Honório would once again be an exemplary worker. That's why he didn't tell his wife the real reason why his friend had left the company. She didn't even ask, in fact.

João Evangelista decided to interrupt his game in order to check out what was happening in the square, even though the spectacle wasn't likely to be any different. It was the same as always, with people searching for their belongings in the midst of all the rubble. Kinaxixi Square was now surrounded by rubble, except for on the right-hand side – that is, if one enters from down the hill – where the market was. In the middle, separated from the rubble by the tarmac, were the Red Cross tents, some of them already torn, which was where the refugees lived. These had transformed the square into a fair of electrical appliances and household goods. Living off the food donated by Mission Aid, and with no real hope of finding another home, they tried to sell their fridges, TVs, furniture, for these things were like rubble inside their tents; they served no function. Many people would come and buy a used electrical appliance for a paltry sum. The street kids had fun with this, and they imitated a certain government-sponsored publicity spot on TV: 'We now have more *economic agents*. The country's growing.'

João didn't find Honório in his tent. But the crowds were so big that he would have had difficulty finding his friend anyway. What he did see were the usual hordes of tourists mesmerized with the sight of each building that fell, and the dozens of foreign specialists who had come to try and find out the causes of the Luanda Syndrome. In one of he tents he discovered what he had predicted to himself: some guy was selling little cards with clumsy drawings of the two buildings still standing: people had to put a cross on the building they thought would fall next.

'That was fast,' João said.

'I was still trying to sell the old set with the third building when it fell,' said the seller. 'I'm preparing a new set. They're doing it all over town. It's a way of making money. It's a pity there are so few buildings left. That'll be the end of business. Unless the beast starts taking on the ones close by.'

The street had now been permanently closed off to traffic. That's why one couldn't see the cars of the *nouveaux-riches*, those latest models with air-conditioning and smoked glass which protect their passengers from the non-stop begging of the street kids, the war amputees and the old people thrown out on to the street by poverty. These rich people are the ones who are doing well, thought João, who did not for a second consider that he was a millionaire businessman himself. They drive past all this misery in their cars refrigerated inside and with music playing at full blast so they won't hear the laments of the beggars who might just upset their spiritual well-being. He avoided two ladies who tried to sell him some TVs, and went over to the other side of the square where the dark water that flowed from the lagoon was carving up the streets all the way towards the road alongside the boulevard, where it was almost impossible to drive in.

'Either they sort out this problem or some day the town centre will be cut off from the rest of the city; it will be a nightmare getting there by car. The water could be channelled towards the bay. It is just a matter of cleaning up the clogged gutters.'

The ones in charge said it wasn't as easy as that, but he couldn't understand why. It was because of the war for sure. According to the official version, the war prevented any solution to the simplest problem. That was it: the war which was taking place a hundred kilometres away prevented the gutters from being unblocked. It was pointless to labour at finding another explanation. Keep faith.

An amputee crossed his path. He didn't have either of his legs and he supported himself with two crutches. 'Give me a little something,' he demanded. Those mutilated by the war had asked and asked, then they gave up asking, and now they demanded. And they looked deep into a person's eyes.

'Look, I've got no money on me.'

'That's it. When I was in the war, I was a hero because I was with the glorious Armed Forces for the Liberation of Angola which was fighting to defend your lives. All the while you were having it good here in the city. Now that I've lost my legs, I'm not a hero any more. I don't even have the right to live. But you still continue to have it good.'

João was going to say that it wasn't his fault, that he wasn't responsible for all that, but what for? It was more prudent to run away. He made tracks, while the other one shouted, 'Band of middle-class prigs, robbers of the people, we'll have you shot by a firing squad yet.' After a few moments of anguish, he ceased to hear him. But it was true in fact: when he left the flat it was just with the intention of going for a walk and he had not brought any money. And what's worse was that he felt he had an obligation to explain to the other man why he couldn't give him any money.

Then all of a sudden he had the strange wish to see the hole from where the water sprung. He crossed the tarmac at the place where it was higher and walked towards the building under construction. He saw some children by the edge of the lagoon. Two boys were fishing for river fish which they sold to the women who were fanning the flames of makeshift coal stoves on the pavement. These in turn roasted the river fish which they sold to the passers-by. They were eaten accompanied by palm oil beans. He moved closer to the boys and it was then that he noticed a girl of about nine or so with her ear almost on the water of the lagoon. He asked the boys:

'What's she doing standing so still like that?'

'Oh, that's Cassandra,' said one of the kids as he threw a line into the water. 'She's doing her pracs, Baba.'

'Doing her pracs? In what?'

'She's doing her pracs in craziness, Baba. She's gone mad. That's what he's trying to say,' said the second one, laughing and pointing to his head with his finger.

João Evangelista moved closer to Cassandra. Next to her was a smaller boy who seemed to be watching her with a forlorn look.

'Can you hear anything?' asked João.

'Can you hear it?' she answered, looking at him with great excitement. And with a sudden hope, João noticed.

'No,' he said.

Cassandra's little face almost shrivelled into sadness. She spoke very softly:

'No one hears it. Then why do you ask?'

She headed towards the unfinished building, and, agile, climbed the wooden ladder that was leaning against it. João turned to the small boy and asked:

'Does she hear things?'

'She says she does. Says it's the Water Spirit. He sings to her. But no one else hears it.'

João gazed at the dark water covered with round leaves and with the papyrus reeds on the edge. Water Spirit? The girl really was doing her pracs. The other boys were right. He returned to the square. For a while he watched the frenzied activity, and he was overpowered by a sadness so great that he had flee to his flat to take refuge in his computer. He walked past the place where, many years before, there had been a huge tree sacred to Kianda, the Water Spirit. He didn't want to think of anything else except how to destroy the well-fortified city of Babylon, the fountain of all luxury.

◆

At last Cassandra was able to find someone who believed her. Old Kalumbo was blind and he had missing teeth. A refugee from the edges of the Kuanza River, he lived on the eighth floor of the building under construction. It was quite a feat getting an old blind man suffering from sclerosis up those makeshift wooden ladders which covered the holes for the cement stairs which had never been completed. Once he was up there the old man never left. It was said that he would die there before he would set foot on the ground again.

'Maybe it's Kianda singing,' he said to Cassandra. 'Kianda manifests himself in many ways. Sometimes it's a ribbon of colours over the water. Other times it's a team of ducks flying in a unique manner. Or it's the whistling of the wind. Why shouldn't it be a song?'

'I saw some drawings of Kianda. Half-woman, half-fish.'

'No,' said old Kalumbo with a sudden vexation. 'That's a white man's thing. That's their mermaid. Kianda is not half-

woman, half-fish. No one has seen him in that form. The settlers stole our soul; they changed everything that was ours, even our way of thinking of Kianda. The result is out there, with this country turned upside down.'

Cassandra listened and she learnt. Each new word she was able to make out from the Water Spirit's song she told the old man. Little by little, the two were able to reconstruct the text. But there were still missing words. To reclaim these words all Cassandra had to do was to move towards the edge and listen. Day and night, any time. Didn't Kianda ever tire of singing?

◆

The fury of the war was worse than ever. It overwhelmed the whole country. Continual bombardments reduced cities to ruins. People fled the cities to seek refuge in the countryside. Here they roamed, searching for food. The ones that couldn't escape from the cities ate cats, rats, dogs, until they had nothing else to chew on. A wind of madness and death swept across the country. In those rare spots where there was no war, the relentless rise in prices impoverished everyone.

'How much lower can we sink?' people asked while standing in the queue, either for the bus, or in front of the store with goods that few of them could afford to buy, or at the hospitals that had neither medicine, cotton nor gauze, or in the schools that had no books and no desks. Luanda was filling up with people fleeing from the war and hunger – at a rate that was as fast as it was suicidal. Thousands of homeless children loitered in the streets, thousands of youths sold and resold things to those that drove past in their cars, countless numbers of war amputees begged for alms at the market. At the same time, important people had luxury cars with smoked glass. No one ever saw their faces. They drove past us and perhaps they didn't

even look so as not to have their consciences made uneasy by
the spectacle of all that misery. João Evangelista didn't want to
think of either the war or the misery. In despair he threw himself
into his game, and forgot all about life.

Chapter Six

The next morning João Evangelista received an unexpected visitor. He almost didn't want to believe what he saw when he opened the door. The door bell rang. It rang and rang, and he didn't pay any attention to it, for it was up to Joana to open the door. It was then that he remembered that Joana had been fired. Much against his will, he got up from his computer desk and went to the door. He was dumbfounded. It was his father, Mateus Evangelista. He had never set foot in his flat. He had done everything to avoid meeting Carmina, who in his eyes was none other than Satan made flesh. He must have had a very strong motive for coming.

'Since you never came to visit your mother again . . . I waited downstairs. I saw your wife leave in her new car – it looks pretty good . . .'

He bade his father sit in the sitting room.

No, he didn't want coffee. He'd already had some. He came to talk. Before, he would sometimes visit João at his work, but they'd told him that he rarely went to work.

'So, I decided to visit you at home. To find out how you're doing.' When they had finished the usual questions and answers about their mutual health there was an uncomfortable silence. João and his father had never been able to speak freely to each other, and this had become worse after his son's marriage to Carmina, which had strained things for good. The old man continued to be the hard, inflexible religious man who was always criticizing João for having lost his head in choosing a heathen for a wife. Mateus Evangelista coughed to clear his throat. It was almost certain he would be making some formal pronouncement.

'I spoke to your mother at length before coming here. Still, it seems to me both necessary and urgent, since the two of you cannot see things in perspective. Why are you waiting to leave this building? Are you waiting for it to fall down? I came to tell you that your room will always be there for you and that it is ready to receive the two of you. The house is not very big, but we can all fit in there. Perhaps your wife won't like it very much, but it's time for us to get to know each other better.'

João couldn't but marvel at all this. Was his father inviting Carmina to come and live in his house? They had to be very worried. It must have been his mother who had convinced the old man, for he was far too stubborn to have had the idea himself.

'Actually, we're thinking of getting another house far away from here. Carmina's been looking, but she hasn't found one yet. But do you really think this building is going to fall down as well?'

'I don't know anything. Only the Lord knows. But since there are so few buildings in this area there's always the possibility that this one will fall too. Maybe not.'

'Actually, no one knows anything. They've been studying it for ages but they haven't reached any conclusions. This is not Kinaxixi any more and this phenomenon just seems to happen in Kinaxixi, but . . .'

'You're wrong. This is still part of old Kinaxixi. It's not in front of the square but it's still Kinaxixi. Your mother will explain it to you. She came to Luanda long before I did. She knows about these old things well.'

That wouldn't mean anything either, thought João. But who can be sure of anything?

'There's one thing I'm certain of,' said Mateus Evangelista. 'This is all tied up with the lack of faith that we see in Angola. We are now living in a society of beggars and thieves. Where are the moral values that will prevent the jealousies, the hatreds, the arbitrary acts, the settling of old scores, the greed? They are gone. There are young people who have never heard of these values. There are young people at school who haven't even learnt that we shouldn't urinate in the street in front of everyone. The only thing people know how to do is to steal. They'll even steal the roof from a hospital – as long as the guard's not there. And who is doing all this? The people, the very people of this country. Because all they can afford to steal is the roof of the hospital which is close by. The ones with power steal much more and they can afford to convict the person who steals from the hospital. The people don't have access to those great businesses and commissions. All they can do is bring down that electricity pylon so they can sell all those bits of metal. Or steal telephone cables to sell the wire. And the country's slowly being destroyed. A brand new school won't even last a year. Because it's the very parents of the students who will steal the desks, the doors, the windows, the corrugated iron sheets. And why do they do all this? Because Angolans have ceased to believe in God.'

'But, Father, never have we seen so many people going to church as now. And sects are springing up everywhere.'

'Does that mean anything at all? False churches, even worse than the papists. Is that the true faith? It would be better if they went to no church at all than go to one of those. All one learns there is how to be a con-artist.'

'Father, you are being a fundamentalist. Is your Church the only true one? Where's the ecumenical spirit?'

'Idle talk. But I came here to offer you our house. Convince your wife. Move today. Your mother will feel much relieved.'

He thanked him for their concern, and said that he would talk to Carmina and that they would decide soon. Mateus Evangelista had accomplished what his sense of duty had compelled him to do. He didn't stay a minute longer in that accursed house. And João didn't insist, for he had interrupted his game at a particularly crucial point.

Ten minutes later the background noise from outside rose a notch higher than the usual purring of the air-conditioning, which indicated that another building had fallen. From his balcony, João could see the huge bulk of the market sprawled on the ground, and the hundreds of people, traders and customers freeing themselves of the dust. It was a two-storey building, so the fall wasn't too big. But the damage was enormous, for the building had occupied an entire block. The truth was that there were no more buildings in the square. The building under construction receded slightly from the line of the square. Now the buildings in the second row would start falling, and would his be included? João Evangelista felt a shiver. He ran to his computer. That is, after he had made a mental note that the time between each successive building falling was being reduced, as though the phenomenon was gaining strength with the bringing down of the first buildings.

When Carmina arrived at lunch-time with a thermos flask with food she had got from a restaurant, for she no longer had a maid, he told her about his parents' offer.

'Nonsense! Why should we go there to put up with that old grumbler? Not even when I'm dead. And it's not as if it solves anything. The problem's not with us. We will fall and hey presto . . . it's our things that'll be the problem. The furniture, the electrical appliances, our clothes. Those things can't all go to your parents' house. There won't be enough space. OK – we'll go, only so as to avoid the fall, which doesn't even hurt by the way, and we'll leave our things here to get stolen by the neighbours, is that it? The solution is to find a house. And finally I've found something interesting.'

João pricked up his ears. Good news?

'They say it's a large house. It's in Samba. The neighbourhood's not good. There are problems with the access roads when it rains, but what the hell. I'm going to see whether we can make a deal. We'll rent this flat to some foreigner and we'll be paid in dollars.'

'Considering we're running away, do you think some foreigner will want to live in this flat?' he said.

'You never know. With foreigners anything is possible, especially if they're white.'

Sometimes he found Carmina's logic disconcerting. But it was pointless to insist. What mattered was to find some sort of place they could move to. Later they could move to a better house in a more dignified neighbourhood. Or perhaps they could build a mansion in Luanda South, that suburb for the *nouveaux-riches*.

After lunch he decided to leave in order to inspect the remains of the market more closely, while Carmina absconded from Parliament in order to try and sort out the house question. He loitered among the remains. He even witnessed some guy stabbing another on account of a radio. He didn't stop to check whether the stabbed man was dead or not. These kinds of scenes were becoming more and more commonplace. He didn't find Honório in the square. He found the same university lecturer with her students gathering data. Scientists never got disheartened; they were forever searching. And the tourists, too, who were photographing and filming everything, enthralled with the lunar landscape into which Kinaxixi had been transformed. They had been warned by the travel agencies and they had everything in duplicate. Because every time they went to the square either a watch or a camera was stolen. Not that anyone was much concerned about this. It was the redistribution of wealth under a different form.

João Evangelista moved over to the other side, and he noticed the water that was running towards the city centre along a valley that had become deeper still. From the news that was being transmitted on TV he knew that the street alongside the boulevard, in an area going all the way from the Baleizão Square up to Nazaré Church, had basically become un-roadworthy. And the way it was getting dug out this was likely to be permanent. One of these days the harbour would be isolated from the rest of the city and that was going to be a problem: how were titbits going to come out? If people already had almost nothing to eat, what was it going to be like when the Mission Aid food got stuck in the harbour? Revolts and more revolts. João had a feeling that things would spread beyond Kinaxixi and strike a mortal blow at the city of Luanda. A foreign company had been hired to drain the water that was coming out of the lagoon, but the workers had not yet started working on it. It was said that because of the emergency of the situation the need for public bidding for the contract had been done away with, and vicious tongues spoke of huge commissions and inflated costs that would make some people get richer. Carmina might have got herself involved in this business – no, she was more into importing beer. It's easier and more profitable. The market for beer does not cease to grow and you get the returns on your investment immediately. A real gold mine.

A child approached him and begged for alms. He handed over a note, knowing full well that it wouldn't solve anything. At least this one would eat a bread roll or a cream doughnut. And the thousands of others? He remembered Cassandra who said she heard strange things in the water. That's where he headed. He didn't find her. Strangely enough there was no one near the lagoon, only the women who sold drinks and river fish on the pavement. But even these women had little space to stand on, for the water had eaten away most of the pavement. That's where the fissure that went all the way down to Baleizão Square started.

His walk had already been over-extended and he returned home as he was beginning to miss his computer. Until Carmina arrived with the news that they both wished for. The house was for sale. It was large, and it had only one drawback, and that was the Samba road which was impossible to drive in during the time of heavy rains. Mind you, that was only once a year. She'd organized everything, except that the price was a little steep. The owner realized that she wanted to move urgently and had upped the price a little. Carmina said they spent two hours arguing over it. She was in a hurry, so she accepted it. Tomorrow they'd legalize the purchase at the public notary. They could move house the day after tomorrow.

That night they slept in fear of being taken by surprise as their flat fell down. Their dreams were full of falls and other accidents. When they woke up they were tired, and anxious about what the day would bring.

Before going to his office, João heard the news on the radio that the government had a plan to solve the question of the buildings that were coming down in Kinaxixi. If only it were possible, he thought to himself. If scientists had not yet discovered the causes, how had the government been able to invent a plan? On the basis of what? The radio announcer didn't explain what this plan was all about. Perhaps it was just a trick to calm the population down; after all, didn't they have a government that was like a daddy who looked after all their interests? Perhaps the news was tied up with the urban myth that João had heard a few days before and which he had not yet had a chance to prove or disprove. The urban myth or rumour went something like this: that more and more of the refugees who lived in the square had taken to dressing exclusively in

92

their birthday suits in order to stroll down the streets of Luanda. People whose minds had become foggy on account of their difficulties and who ended up stepping inside the world of dreams. It seemed as if there was an abnormally high rate of such people among those who had formerly resided in the buildings of Kinaxixi, and who were now convinced they were in Berlin's Hallensee and became Luanda's own nudists, much to the indignation of right-thinking people. It was said that they weren't psychological wrecks, but rather that it was a way of protesting against the passivity of the authorities which did little to sort out their basic problems.

'To be honest, yesterday when I went to the square I didn't notice more naked people than usual, but I wasn't paying any attention to it either. Perhaps Honório could explain it me.' He remembered that Carmina had been entrusted to find a job for his friend, but the worries of the last few days had made him put this issue to the back of his mind. He had to remind his wife of the promise she had made. He threw himself at the game with all his heart.

◆

Meanwhile, in the building under construction Cassandra was telling old Kalumbo the words of the song which she had finally been able to make out. It was Kianda's lament, just as they had previously guessed. He complained that for centuries he had lived in perfect happiness in his lagoon until men decided to drain his lagoon and put cement and sand and tar on top of it, and build a square and buildings all around it. Kianda felt stifled with all that weight on top of him. He couldn't swim. And then he revolted against it. He sang. He sang until all the buildings fell down, one by one, slowly. That was what Kianda wished for. And that was what Cassandra told old Kalumbo.

'We should warn the people in the building that it's about to fall down.'

'Even though it's not finished?' she asked.

'Even though.'

'No one's going to believe me. No one's ever listened to me. And why should we warn them if we've got nowhere else to go?'

Cassandra didn't warn anyone. As for the words, she heard nothing that was new. She spent the whole day by the edge of the lagoon, listening to the song, which to her sounded less and less sad but more and more victorious.

◆

Later in the afternoon, after Carmina had given him the news that the deeds had been signed and that the house was legally theirs and that she was going to rent a truck and hire removal men to move their things early the next morning, João received a visit from Honório. The shock of seeing him almost threw him back, right through the open window of the sitting room. Honório was completely naked, which gave credence to the rumour João had not wanted to believe. He looked to all sides; he wasn't sure if he was going to allow his friend to enter his home under these conditions. Luckily Carmina wasn't at home, but she could turn up any time and throw one of her usual fits.

'Are you surprised? It's the new fashion in Kinaxixi. It's taking on. The homeless in Kinaxixi are protesting against a government which does nothing for them. Nakedness is our new national garb, the one that's in accordance with the standard of living of our people. We can't even walk around in a loincloth. A loincloth is a middle-class luxury.'

'Are you heeding the advice of the poet who said that we shall return to our traditions?'

'No. It's got nothing to do with traditionalism. Especially given that our ancestors walked around in loincloths, raffia skirts, and so on. It really is a protest. Nakedness is the only garb compatible with the poverty into which we have sunk.'

'I heard that more and more people were walking around naked, but I didn't know it had reached the proportions of a political movement.'

'No, it's a civic movement. It's a question of civic coherence. How can we walk around fully clothed if they take everything away from us and refuse to help us? Every day our currency is devalued, the prices of goods rise, no one can work because salaries are the only things in this country which don't rise. Isn't it a shameful luxury to adorn yourself with clothes, even if they are the rags from some filthy cloth? It's showing off your wealth and it cannot be tolerated. We haven't moved to action yet. Because we're going to start taking off the clothes of the people who walk around in the streets.'

'But if you do that you'll be punished.'

'How? The mad have always walked the streets naked and no one's ever arrested them. Are they going to arrest us? There are thousands of us. And then they've got to prove that we are not mad. And honestly, you've got to admit that we are mad. This is a symptom of madness. A conscious madness, perhaps.'

João had become very confused of late with what was happening in his life and that of others. He had no arguments to use against Honório's ideas. But he tried to get his friend to see reason.

'I'm not sure if this is good for you. Carmina's been talking to her friends and she assured me that she would find you a job where you'll earn in dollars. But if you arrive at work all naked . . .'

'I'm very grateful for your wife's concern. If she finds a job I might rethink. When the time comes I'll decide if I should change social class. But at this moment I belong to the class of the naked. There's now a class struggle in society, and it's between the naked and the fully-clothed. They tried to kill Marx before his time and now he's on his way back to avenge himself. And don't you go down into the square with your clothes on because we are going to start tearing off people's clothes.'

'To walk around naked in protest, well, it's shocking at first sight, but if you were to consider it carefully you would have to admit there's some logic to it. Deep down it's a moralistic movement. Now, if you attack people, if you destroy people's property – their clothes – then you'll be giving the police a pretext to act against you. Is that an intelligent thing to do?'

'Perhaps not. Maybe it's too soon. We've got members of our civic movement in other parts of the city. Don't think it's only happening in Kinaxixi. In no time we'll be millions and no one fights against millions. Then, yes, that will be the moment to impose social equality by force, that is, to tear off the clothes of the rich.'

It wasn't the same Honório speaking. Before, he used to be the timid, hard-working, conformist worker – the model party activist. After his ill-fated experience, he went through a short, dishonest period – a peccadillo, really. But now he was different, headstrong, as though high on new ideas. Could low-key Honório make a leader? And he *would* become a leader if the fashion really took hold. And what's worse, the climate helped. One can be comfortable in this heat only if one is naked . . .

'But does this fashion apply equally to women, or is it just a male movement?'

'Honestly, João, how could you think that a civic uprising of this nature would be restricted to men only? Actually, women are the ones who are the most enthusiastic about this whole thing. If you go to the square you'll find hundreds of naked women.'

'I haven't left the house yet today.'

'Then you are losing out. Actually, by locking yourself up here you're allowing life to slip through your fingers. Everyone chooses his form of madness. Ours at least is fun. It's also a collective effort and it implies solidarity. And it's a positive thing, because the government will be too ashamed to do nothing.'

'But Honório, you are going to get the Churches hounding you down. They'll accuse you of undermining public morals, etc, etc . . .'

'All Churches get very cosy with the powers that be. That's why it would be normal for them to shriek against a movement as radical and genuine as ours. But it doesn't matter. The revolt will be so huge that they'll be the ones to lose out if they turn against us. Actually, they're hesitating. They haven't taken a position. And don't suppose that they don't know what's going on. The Churches aren't as out-of-touch as you are.'

He had to admit that his friend was right in criticizing the way in which he had alienated himself. Sometimes his conscience would prick him and he would force himself to go out into the street, or go to work. But the intention was more to put aside the computer for a short while rather than anything else. It didn't spring from a desire to face reality. But he felt that he was in danger when he was out on the street. He couldn't really define it. He didn't know where it came from. But there was danger all around him. Only at home did he feel safe. Especially at his desk, immersed in the keyboard of his computer; that way he could forget the world out there, which was becoming more and more aggressive and unpredictable.

'And how are you organized? Do you have a leadership, a central committee?'

'No way. Everything's informal. The most active ones, the ones who are the most interested, discuss things and take

97

decisions. Whoever comes to meetings is allowed to take part. They're open to everyone. We don't have rigid structures. They end up by preventing all initiatives and by oppressing the members. Political parties have become prisons of that kind, and we are not a political party. We want to foment a rebellion that will force the State to ignore the dictates of the IMF which are making us all the more poor to the benefit of the foreigners and some corrupt people. That's why this movement has to start from the initiative of the people. They cannot be strait-jacketed by parties that pursue objectives which just have to do with their own power. In fact, many of us have come to the conclusion that this thing about parties is all very well for Europe, for that's where they were invented, but that here we need our own ways of organizing. We need to dare ourselves to think with our own heads.'

Actually, they seemed to have a political programme, an ideology. João Evangelista felt that his love for political theory was being reawakened. Wasn't their ideology very similar to the one espoused by those who became known as utopian or anarchistic socialists? Honório did not cease to amaze him. It's true that during his days as an activist for the party that was now the ruling party he had always taken part in the Ideology Meetings during which they discussed theory, and that at one time he had even considered doing one of the party's graduate courses. He had read all the classics of Marxism. In a sense he'd had the necessary training and that would serve him well were he to head a civic movement. No sooner had João said this, than he had to reap the whirlwind:

'I lead nothing at all. What kind of mentality have you been left with? The mentality of petty-minded people who can't look at anything without thinking of authority and authoritarianism. The movement is a spontaneous one. I don't even know who had the idea about us going around naked. And many of the ideas that we've developed have arisen out of regular discussions. It's a genuine mass movement. It's not like the ones you know from the past which were always cooked up in some office or other and then, only afterwards, would they call on the masses to give their support. This arose from the masses and no one's going to control it and make use of it. We – *the whole lot of us* – we won't allow it. We are creating history because we are inventing our own ways. It's time to stop copying our formulas from overseas. We have to invent our own methods for the struggle.'

Here was a popular leader; no longer was he a naked man in another person's house, but he was on stage in some public square making a speech that would inflame the masses. João Evangelista didn't say a word. His friend said goodbye, saying: 'Take a walk through Kinaxixi. You'll see the revolutionary fervour of your youth.'

João was left with the feeling that the movement was going to come to a bad end, with bloodshed, because their ideas were too new, too daring. Had they created their own ideas and methods of fighting? Didn't they give a fig about the moulds and formulas of the countries in the northern hemisphere? Too subversive; and destined for failure and mourning. But it probably is rather pleasant to walk around the streets naked, your body cool all over, and not be in the least concerned about what other people think. The freedom of a bird. Or of a fish.

Carmina arrived home not long after. It was as though she were sitting on a hurricane. João shuddered. He thought perhaps Operation New House had not come through. But that wasn't the reason why. She was livid with what she had seen and heard in Kinaxixi Square.

'When they first told me yesterday I didn't want to believe it. And today I didn't even notice it at first. But now I've seen it. It's unthinkable. Did you know that there are thousands, and I mean thousands, of naked peole in the square and in the streets? And it's not only in Kinaxixi. I saw them in Vila Alice. And they've told me that in Rangel and Sambizanga they've done it, too. They've all thrown away their clothes and they are dancing in the streets naked.'

'Honório was here. He told me. He was naked.'

'He came here? Naked? In my house?'

'He denies it, but I think he's one of the leaders. Do you know why this has taken on?'

'Some subversive movement. That's all it can be.'

It was as though Carmina had heard everything. That's what they call political scent. Of course, it's not infallible. When she declared that the falling of the buildings was the result of sabotage, it was obvious that she was clearly in the wrong, but now she hit the nail on the head.

'The government's not doing anything for the refugees. It's a form of protest. A civic movement.'

'We'll give them civic movement. The army's moving in and all this getting fresh will come to an end. A few broken skulls and this fashion will be old news.'

She picked up her cellphone, her latest acquisition and a symbol of her status in society.

'What are you going to do, Carmina?'

'It should be obvious. I'm going to phone someone to stop this immoral monkeying around. Have you ever seen children looking at their naked parents? It's a scandal. It's unethical.'

'Stop it. It's far more unethical to steal food from the people and do nothing to stop it. It's a peaceful protest. They're not harming anyone. Stop your excessive morality. What's important is what's really at stake: no one's worried about the refugees, no one's worried about the thousands of kids who live out on the street, no one's worried about the men mutilated in the war. This kind of revolt was bound to blow up. And this is quite original, in fact. And peaceful. You're not offended because they're naked, it's because they're criticizing your government.'

Carmina put away her cellphone. João thought, 'Sometimes I am still able to control Carmina, but at this precise moment how many others are phoning the authorities and calling for blood in the name of public decency? The same ones who shamelessly steal from the State. Their *pudeur* doesn't extend as far as theft.'

His wife went to give vent to her rage in a positive manner: she decided to make dinner. Rather that. And João threw himself against the Romans who had taken refuge in the Australian continent, in what was also an obvious misrepresentation of time and place. If he controlled them he would be able to control the world in an even shorter time span. His only hope was that Carmina would take longer making dinner so that he would have time to finish the game, and thus make sure the best scores he had ever obtained would be placed next to his name.

There was an odd musical sound – a shake. João Evangelista felt that he had been hurled into space. He grabbed his computer and tried to press the key that would function as a catapult against the Romans, but with a cut in the power supply the screen went down. And in the vortex of that fall he saw that Carmina was on top of him, her arms stretched out as they tried to hold him, her eyes full of terror and love. He saw objects, tables, bricks, people swirling in the air as if in slow motion, and a cat with his fur on end and with his paws ready to land as cats know how. João Evangelista did not see

that the building under construction was also disintegrating to the sound of musical notes. But old blind Kalumbo was flying, transformed into a bird. The bricks, the lamps, the stoves, mats, pots were all coming down. Cassandra felt the call that was coming from the waters of the lagoon, and she flapped her arms

101

*as though she were swimming and she guided her fall by diving
into the water. Gone forever. Now that it had reached its full
strength, the song burst through the thickness of the water and
flooded the city, telling all of Kianda's until-then-secret wish.*

Before he landed on the ground, João saw the whole of Kinaxixi
Square full of naked people applauding at the Water Spirit's
latest feat. The computer fell on top of him, and then the piles
of rubble and the cement dust. There he remained, embracing
his computer, with no wish to leave the place. They would
conduct searches to get him out, but later. That's also why he
did not see

*the multi-coloured ribbons that illuminated Luanda's night sky
arising from Kinaxixi lagoon and from all along the trenches
carved out by the water. And how they ran down Rua da
Missão and the cobblestone walk that led to the boulevard
roadway and continued along this road all the way up to
Baleizão, together with all the water that had accumulated, to
form a huge tidal wave which flooded out the entire central
avenue and moved on to collide with the causeway under the
fortress, a causeway the Portuguese had filled up with rubble
and stones so that the island would cease to be an island, and
could become instead a peninsula that was connected to the
African continent by an isthmus of stones and cement. The tidal
wave with the rainbow-coloured ribbons hovering above it
demolished the isthmus, and the water from the lagoon was
mixed with the salt water and the living colours spread all the
way to Corimba now that the Island of Luanda was once again
an island and Kianda, free at long last, had earned for himself
the high seas.*

Luanda, 1994–5